GOLEM

GOLEM

GREG VILK

ricochet

Los Angeles

This book contains hidden messages, which includes the chapter script.

Cover and book design by Greg Vilk

ISBN 0-9772189-0-2

Published by Ricochet Press
www.ricpress.com
Los Angeles

More information about the book at
www.gregvilk.com

LCCN 2005933994

Printed in the United States of America

Printing series:
2-14-2/4-4-2/5-7-2/9-10-9/6-22-1/4-6-2/
10-7-10/4-4-3/4-6-4/8-11-5/9-10-4/2-4-2/2-11-9/
9-4-2/11-7-1/5-5-3/4-22-6/9-3-5/11-9-6

Acknowledgments

My words of gratitude go to Heather Lodge for her dedicated and thorough editing work. I also wish to thank Stel Pavlou and Jeremy Robinson for their early feedback.

The Old Malachim script was inspired by the Alphabet Synthesis Machine, an online interactive artwork created for PBS by Golan Levin, Jonathan Feinberg, and Cassidy Curtis.

"Half of man's wisdom rests in knowing where it ends."

Corpus Hermeticum
3rd century

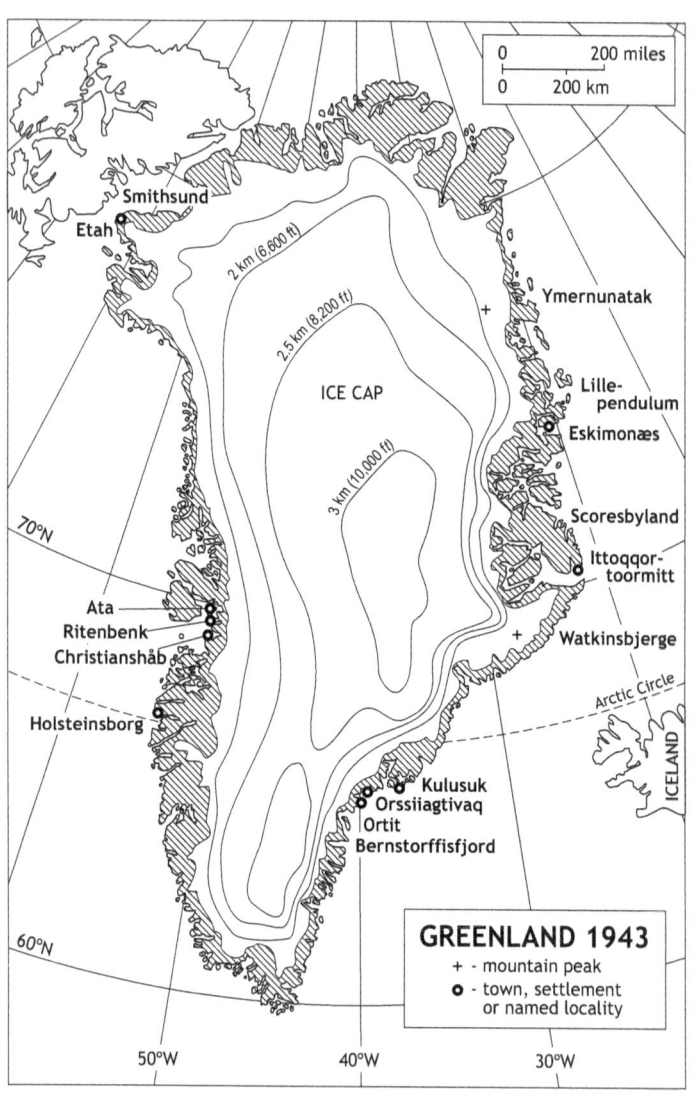

200 miles

200 km

Smithsund

Etah

2 km (6,600 ft)

2.5 km (8,200 ft)

Ymernunatak

+

ICE CAP

Lille-
pendulum

Eskimonæs

3 km (10,000 ft)

Scoresbyland

70°N

Ittoqqor-
toormitt

Ata

Ritenbenk

+

Watkinsbjerge

Christianshåb

Arctic Circle

Holsteinsborg

ICELAND

Kulusuk

Orssiiagtivaq

Ortit

Bernstorffisfjord

60°N

GREENLAND 1943

+ - mountain peak

o - town, settlement
or named locality

50°W

40°W

30°W

PROLOGUE

Northeast Greenland, November 1942

THE INUIT MOTHER stepped out of the igloo and frowned at a young boy romping with the huskies.

"Get back in right now, Sauri!"

The boy sprinted toward her.

"How many times do I need to tell you? If you spoil the dogs, they don't work the hitch!" She grabbed the boy by his anorak and dragged him into the igloo.

Greenland was halfway through the polar night. The sun slumbered six degrees below the horizon, close enough to cast a faint glow behind the distant glaciers. High up above arched the dark firmament, kindled by the flickering aurora. The small Inuit village nestled in a snow plain, sheltered from biting gales by a cluster of hillocks. The four families who lived here had trekked this far north in search of seal, which had grown scarce south of Scoresby Sund. Surrounding them was a perfect desolation. The bleak snow plain stretched west all the way to the horizon. To the east the North Atlantic lay frozen, its scattered, towering icebergs trapped offshore like a herd of dinosaurs on their way to extinction. The closest trace of civilization was a small hunting station in Eskimonæs, 100 miles to the south. The hunters who normally wintered there had just been drafted into the Greenland Army—a grandiose name for a few dozen sled teams armed with rusty 1914 Mausers.

The igloos glowed orange through their icy mortar, lit from inside by small fires. In the boy's igloo, his family crouched around a steaming pot, slurping *oogruk,* or walrus broth, from small bowls. The seal-oil fire that heated the pot was so small that it made a better lamp than a hearth. Firewood was scarce in Greenland and burning a bonfire inside a snow house had never been a good idea. A dank, fatty smell came from the sealskins that had been soaked in train oil for waterproofing and hung up to dry. The grown-ups ate in silence, savoring the broth. The boy slurped out loud with amusement, his chubby face cocooned inside his anorak.

"They can hear you in Iceland," his mother said, squinting at him.

"It's hot, Mom!"

She reached over, picked up his bowl, slapped a fistful of snow into his hand, and put the bowl on top of it.

"There."

All of a sudden the broth in the pot rippled as a tremor shook the ground. The family exchanged puzzled glances. A low, rumbling noise droned in a distance, growing louder and louder. They darted out of the igloo, knocking over the pot.

The huskies howled and snapped their teeth at the surroundings. The other villagers had come out as well, and now stood in tense silence. Oil lamp in hand, the boy's father peered around. Nothing but a hilly landscape tinted blue by the aurora.

Then a massive, boxy shape emerged from behind a hillock and rumbled toward the village.

"Hide! Hide! Quick!" an elder ordered, waving his arms at the others.

"Sauri! Get over here right now!" the mother yelled, her frightened eyes on the boy.

The Inuit hid behind their igloos. Huddled together, they watched the object draw close. It was a massive battle tank in polar camouflage, its engine huffing from exertion. The turret was marked with German army insignia and the unit name *Kommando Thule*. The tank commander, visible in dark silhouette, stood motionless in the turret hatch, his hands clawing the handles, his head held firm against the harsh wind.

The villagers gaped in amazement as the tank rolled on toward the igloos. When it was only a few yards away, the boy shrieked. The tank commander was dead, his body frozen in a standing pose. His ashen face, sucked dry like a mummy by the Arctic gales, was twisted in a rictus of horror, as if he'd glimpsed hell before he died. The Inuit shrank back, aghast.

The tank's engine choked, running out of steam. The tank rolled over a few sleds, crushing them like matchsticks, then plowed into the nearest igloo and stopped. The engine gave out its last gasp.

A deep silence followed. Even the wind let up a bit, as if perplexed by what had just happened. Finally, the villagers breathed again. They stepped gingerly out of hiding and surrounded the tank. A murmur of dread rolled through the crowd. Three German soldiers lay on their backs behind the turret, frozen and twisted in agony. One firmly clutched a crucifix in his freeze-dried hand. Their shriveled eyes peered into the darkness, transfixed by some unseen danger.

An Inuit hunter spoke up in Greenlandic Danish, his voice quivering.

"Is anyone alive?"

Silence. The hunter inched toward the tank and tapped on the armor with his bone-tipped harpoon. Something slipped out of a German's hand, clattered on the armor, and landed in the snow. It was a military logbook marked with a German army eagle. The hunter picked it up and flipped through the pages filled with orderly handwriting. The last pages were glued together with a splotch of frozen blood. The hunter tweezed them apart. He had no way of understanding the final entry scrawled across the page in big, screaming letters:

God Help Us All

CHAPTER I

Guadalcanal, November 1942

BLACK PALLS of smoke towered above the hills like funeral pyres lit by giants. The air was thick with a burning stench. Distant explosions echoed among the hilltops as though vengeful gods had commanded every volcano on the island to erupt in unison. For the last few months, the frontline had moved to and fro in gory leaps: hilltop to hilltop, foxhole to foxhole, pillbox to pillbox. The Japanese fought hard and mean, spurred into battle rage by the daily incantations of the ancient Bushido mantra *Death Before Surrender!* Each day they sent suicide squads to blow up P-38 fighters right off American airstrips. Hyakutake, the hard-nosed Japanese commander, was already practicing his conqueror's speech to be delivered on the first Australian beachhead he'd take.

U.S. Army jeeps, encased in shells of dried mud, hauled along ancient dirt roads, winding their way around treacherous ravines. Sweat-drenched Marines plodded along in grumbling columns. Damn the Japanese. Damn the HQ. Damn the mosquitoes. For every casualty of war, malaria killed two.

Amid the bombed-out moonscape stood a badly damaged Spanish colonial hacienda, its red roof tiles scattered around like a shrapnel wound. A fat hillock shielded it from gunfire. The scorched walls bore witness to the battle that had taken place here just days ago. Draped across the roof was a large U.S. flag. The makeshift sign posted near the entrance read: *14th Corps HQ, Henderson Field.* The front yard bustled with Army grunts.

Five battle-scarred jeeps skidded to a halt before the entrance, trailing a dust cloud. The soldiers in the yard stopped and gaped on, intrigued. Even on this battlefield the jeeps were quite a sight: riddled by bullets, scorched, hot oil spraying from an engine half blown-off by a mortar shell. Stenciled on the door panels was a glowering skull and the slogan: *Run Silent, Run Deep, Run'em Over.*

A platoon of Rangers piled out of the jeeps and stretched their arms. They were filthy and bloodied, as if fresh from fierce combat.

Leading them was Captain Plutarch M. Leash. He was 34; his eyes ten years younger, his face ten years older. A swath of ash-blond stubble blanketed his cheeks from ear to ear. His face looked restrained, almost melancholic, yet hiding deep in his green eyes was the telltale glow of a man who had just scored big. In his arms he clutched a battered briefcase with a pair of broken handcuffs dangling from its handle.

Right next to him stood Sergeant La Costa, known as Hitch. A lazy sneer played on his lips, as he chewed without mercy on some poor toothpick. He had muscles like an oil derrick, his face melting straight into a neckless chest. His forehead sweated under a tartan bandana. An open bag of toothpicks peeked out from his rolled-up sleeve; a ten-inch Bowie knife hung menacingly from his hip.

Beside Hitch towered Sergeant DeClerk, nicknamed Eiffel for his soaring, bottom-heavy frame, which defied basic rules of anatomy. His racoonish eyes peered around with suspicion. Framing his face was a crop of dark hair so oily, it refused to flutter in the wind. A white-fringed gyrfalcon with a deadly stare perched on a leather patch strapped to his shoulder.

Hitch glanced at his watch with glee.

"The whole stunt in forty-eight hours with an hour to spare. Next time bet on horses."

"Don't rub it in, Hitch," Eiffel's voice was nasal, as if he'd had peas stuck in his nostrils since he was a kid.

Defeat in his eyes, Eiffel pulled out a twenty and handed it to Hitch. He eyed Hitch's toothpick with disgust. "At least you didn't drool when you smoked."

Hitch flashed a triumphant grin, unfazed. He held the bill up and showed it to the Rangers.

"The brew's on Eiffel!"

The Rangers cheered.

"Come on," Leash said. "He's waiting."

Leash, Hitch, and Eiffel dusted off their fatigues and started toward the HQ building. The soldiers in the yard stepped back in quiet respect.

Leash took an eager notice. His rep among the ranks was solid as ever. The quiet sort of flattery had always worked for him the best. He was beginning to expect it.

Leash strolled with a measured gait, putting on a mask of indifference. Eiffel waddled nearby with an odd, apprehensive gait, like Donald Duck crossing a minefield.

Hitch marched along, trying hard to cover up his slight limp with a cocky swagger. Leash knew the secret. A few months back a bullet had licked Hitch at the ankle. Hitch kept mum; the limp could have him thrown out of the unit on medical grounds. Leash closed his eyes on it. A pair of healthy legs had nothing on Hitch.

They entered the HQ building and approached a room with a makeshift sign scrawled on the door: *Col.*

Vischer, Military Intelligence. The young corporal on duty sprang to his feet, awe in his eyes. He promptly opened the door and showed Leash in.

"Come in, sir! He's waiting!"

Leash, Eiffel, and Hitch entered the room.

The shabby ruin had once been an elegant study. Colonel Vischer — fiftyish, half-bald, with a rim of buzz-cut, black hair and a no-nonsense stare — sat at the paper heap he called his desk. Maps of Guadalcanal hung tacked to the empty bookshelves. A truckload of torn, Spanish-era books lay scattered on the floor, as if they'd been shoved straight off the shelves.

Leash took this in with a calm gaze. He knew full well why the books had hit the floor. A few months ago, Vischer's pregnant daughter had run away with a writer. Better to take it out on books than a bottle.

"I don't care how you level the field!" Vischer rasped into the phone, his voice corroded by cigars. "You dumped the ordnance, you clean it up!"

He slammed the receiver onto the cradle. The corporal cowered, his meek voice down to a whisper.

"Captain Leash, sir."

Vischer glanced up. The anger faded from his face.

"First Rangers' Special Op Commando, sir." Leash saluted Vischer. "Mission accomplished."

He approached Vischer's desk and calmly set down the battered briefcase.

"The code books of the Japanese 17th army."

He sounded so at ease, he might as well have been handing out chocolate cookies. The nonchalance he'd been rehearsing for years was his second nature by now; he could even play down a triumph as big as this one. But he watched Vischer closely, sizing up his reaction.

Vischer reached across the desk and eagerly opened the briefcase. Leash's face brightened with a smile.

Home run.

"Careful, sir. We've just defused the booby trap."

Vischer peeked inside with burning curiosity. The briefcase was laden with explosives, their wires cut and pulled apart for safety. From in between the wiring, Vischer removed a notebook. He flipped through the pages filled with number tables and Japanese characters. His eyes sparked with excitement. He ran his fingers across the notebook's spine like a boy caressing a Christmas gift. Then he frowned, looked at his hand, and winced. The notebook was smeared with blood. He looked up at Leash, puzzled.

"Their code officer tried to blow it up in the last second," Leash said.

"What stopped him?"

Hitch wiped blood off his knife's blade with a slow ostentation. "A sudden numbness in his hands, sir."

Eiffel let out a subdued chuckle. Vischer eyed Hitch's knife with a strange mixture of respect and disgust.

"Glad we scooped you out of that Ohio jail, Hitch. I knew your knife had a higher calling."

Hitch smiled. He seemed unfazed by the backhanded compliment. Vischer picked up the phone.

"Get in here, Otis."

The young corporal popped his head in.

"Get it to Ciphers, on the double." Vischer tossed him the notebook. "The codes are still hot."

The corporal caught the notebook and was gone.

Vischer put on a fatherly grin of approval and approached the Rangers.

"How are you doing, Johanna?" He smiled to Eiffel's falcon. "Did'ya nab Hirohito?"

The bird shot him an indifferent stare, too busy grooming its wings.

Vischer shook hands with the Rangers, one by one. "Kudos. You, men, put the *one* in *number one.*"

Leash soaked up the praise, but he certainly wasn't going to show it. "Thank you, sir. The two-week leave you promised gave the men wings."

Vischer bit his lips and paused with unease, as if about to broach a tough subject.

"Sorry, Captain. The leave will have to wait."

Leash, Hitch, and Eiffel looked at each other. The news hit them like a left hook.

"Get your men to the briefing room," Vischer said. "You got yourself a new stint." He headed out, leaving behind a gallery of pained faces.

Hitch took off his helmet. From inside he pulled out a photo of a six-year-old, pig-tailed girl on a swing. He gave it a tender kiss. "So long, Emily. Nice to *not* see you again."

He sighed, put the photo back in, and fixed Leash with a bitter stare. "When will this game end, sir?"

"What game?"

Hitch swiveled his head around, pointing at the world at large.

"The war."

"When the cards are all played out."

They stood in silence for a moment. Then they followed Vischer out of the room, dragging their feet in resignation.

Leash played with a pencil as he looked around the briefing room. It was an ex-dining hall that had surely known better times. Below the vaulted ceiling hung two sad remnants of colonial chandeliers. Silverware lay scattered on the floor. The Rangers sat at a mahogany table the size of an aircraft carrier, whispering between themselves. Their curious eyes were on Vischer, who stood at the head of the table, getting ready to give a briefing. A projection screen stretched on the wall behind him.

Seated nearby was a poker-faced civilian. He was in his forties, with brown hair parted so meticulously, he may as well have used calipers. In his herringbone suit and worn loafers, he could pass for a harmless drudge from a small-town bank. Leash wasn't fooled for a second. The man's dagger-eyed stare belonged to a man who meant business.

Vischer raised his hand, ready to speak. The chatter in the room died down. Vischer pointed to the civilian.

"This is Section Chief Ramsey from the War Department, Enemy Weapons Research. Mr. Ramsey?"

Ramsey got up. Without any further introduction, he snapped his fingers at someone in the back. The lights went out and a projected slide lit up the screen. It showed the photo of a bookish, wheelchair-bound man in his sixties. He wore horn-rim glasses and a threadbare, elbow-patched pullover that could only belong to a lifetime academic. Ramsey spoke in a measured, matter-of-fact tone.

"Six months ago, a Yale professor vanished during his trip to Turkey. Three months ago, our agents saw him in Hamburg, being taken aboard a plane headed for the North Atlantic. We suspect he was kidnapped to help the Nazis develop a top-secret weapons project."

The slide changed to show an aerial photo.

"A few weeks ago, a recon plane took these over a remote place in northeast Greenland called Thule Bay."

The photo showed an Arctic coastline. A large military base sprawled on the shore. Four massive silos towered above the base like a nest of mammoth ostrich eggs. To the east, the base opened onto a large, frozen bay. A curving mountain range shielded the base from other directions.

"Looks like a German U-boat fuel depot," Ramsey said. "But look at the heaps of dug-out ice."

He pointed out a detail in the photo. Off to the side, in a secluded section, rose a few large heaps of ice blocks.

"Looks like a massive dig. We suspect it's the underground weapons labs."

The slide changed.

"Last week, we took these pictures."

The photo showed a close-up of the same base. The place now looked like a city after a riot. Tanks and trucks huddled abandoned by the roadside. Equipment and debris lay scattered in disarray everywhere.

"Abandoned vehicles. The power is out. The radio is dead. No signs of the crew. Something happened there."

The lights came back on. Ramsey locked a firm gaze with the Rangers. His tone was tough and determined.

"I was charged with a mission to rescue the professor and destroy the weapons labs. I chose you, men, because you're the best special ops squad since the angel Gabriel. We'll get a guide who knows the local ice caves. One branch ends inside the base. When we're done, a plane will pick us up. Any questions?"

Silence fell on the room as the Rangers digested the information. Leash drilled his eyes into Ramsey.

"Sir, what exactly are those weapons?"

"I can't tell you, Captain, for security reasons. What I can say is that no one has ever seen anything like it." He paused for effect. "Prepare yourself for the unknown."

The Rangers traded puzzled glances. Hitch raised his hand like a first-grader, a mock concern on his face.

"Sir, will I need my bathing suit?"

The Rangers hee-hawed.

Leash could never quite understand Hitch's constant need for clowning. Maybe a big mouth is what it took for Hitch to survive that Ohio jail. Or childhood, for that matter.

Vischer didn't look amused. "Save the giggles till you get there, Hitch. It's polar night in Greenland. Minus twenty and half dark. The sun won't show up for a few more weeks."

The Rangers grumbled among themselves.

"The colonel is right," Ramsey said. "The eastern coast is a frozen nightmare."

The slide changed. It now showed a map of Greenland. Ramsey pointed to the ice cap.

"The glaciers push toward the ocean, dragging along ice blocks and moraines, which can be used for hideouts." He pointed to the coastal waters. "The shelf is now frozen solid. The frost pressure tears the sea-ice inside out and squeezes out ice plates twenty feet in height."

Wow. Nice and cozy. Key West had just slipped to No. 2 on Leash's list of top holiday spots. He frowned and scratched his forehead.

"Sir, I'm not that up on politics, but won't we get busted for trespassing? Last time I checked, Greenland was a Danish colony."

"That's right, Captain. *Was.* Now it isn't. When Germans took over Denmark, the bailiff of Greenland, a fellow by the name of—" Ramsey searched his papers, "Eske Brun sent out feelers to Washington and signed an accord with the Department of State. The place is now our wartime protectorate. But that's all on paper."

He tapped on the projected map. "This is reality. A giant maze of fjords and islands. You can hide a base there and no one will know for months."

"Months?" Leash lifted his eyebrows. "That's more than enough time to put up a defense system."

"Or booby-trap the whole place," Eiffel said.

Ramsey's gaze ran across the faces.

"And that's where you come in, gentlemen."

The Rangers murmured among themselves. Vischer raised his hand to get their attention. His voice came down a notch, as if anticipating a bad reaction.

"One more thing. You're taking along a civilian."

He glanced off to the side. The Rangers followed his gaze. Someone was sitting in a chair in a dark corner of the room, face hidden in shadows. Barely visible in the light was a pair of female legs in beige panty hose with a back seam. The legs sure got the Rangers' attention. They hadn't seen a back seam for quite a while.

"Miss Benedict?" Vischer addressed the woman.

May Benedict, a brunette in her late twenties, rose from her seat in the shadows and strutted into the light, her heels clicking on the hardwood floor. The Rangers' eyes promptly looked her over, head to toe. With her wire-rim glasses, French braids, plaid cardigan and a prim skirt, she looked like she'd just been released from some locked-up nunnery known as a New England girls' college. She was comely; a slight skew of the cheekbones only lent her face a stronger punch. A necklace of strangely oversized corals coiled tight around her neck, as if deep down she had a secret wish to choke herself. With a slight pout of her lips and an aloof gaze, she gave off the air of someone entitled to better company than this.

Leash's face soured. He could tell her kind a mile away. An ice queen in training. He crossed his arms and fixed Vischer with a malcontent gaze.

"Sir, can I speak frankly?"

Vischer nodded.

"Sir, you know that civilians endanger—"

"She's coming, Leash."

Vischer's voice cracked like a bullwhip. May's face reddened and tensed up. She looked hurt.

"I don't . . . I really don't . . ." She bit her lips like she was holding back.

Vischer raised his hand in a calming gesture. "No need to explain yourself, Miss Benedict."

Leash opened his mouth for a riposte. Vischer shot him a firm stare. "She's *in,* Captain. As *in* as *in* can be."

Leash sighed and reclined in his seat with a dour face. "Can I ask who she is?" he said.

Vischer hesitated and sneaked a glance at Ramsey. Ramsey nodded.

"A linguist."

The Rangers looked at Vischer confused, as if he'd just switched over to Swahili.

"A *what*-guist?" Hitch said.

"Ph.D. in ancient languages."

The Rangers eyed each other, baffled.

"Sir, what kinda mission is this?" Hitch said. "Did the Nazis kidnap the Pope and he speaks only Latin?"

He got a solid round of giggles from the ranks. Vischer sighed, as if too tired to call Hitch down. Ramsey leaned over toward Hitch and fixed him with a deadly serious stare. His words hit hard like hailstones.

"Sergeant, when push comes to shove, she might be the best weapon you've got."

The chuckles in the room quickly died down. The Rangers drilled their eyes into Ramsey, as if hoping to extract the elusive meaning behind his words.

"That will be all." Ramsey gathered his papers and marched out of the room.

"Get some rest now," Vischer said. "Your plane takes off in three days."

He headed out in Ramsey's footsteps. The Rangers gazed at each other, surrounded by the air of silent mystery.

Leash lay on a bunk in his quarters. The room was dark, save for a small lamp next to his bed. He rolled over to rest his head on his right arm. His left elbow had lately been giving him this annoying, numb feeling for no apparent reason. In his hands he held a folder labeled *Mission Background,* stamped all over with State Department seals and *Top Secret* warnings. Leash hated these things. He could already picture some drab government drone poring through libraries and diplomatic mail to sweat out these bone-dry treatises. Leash sighed and opened the folder.

"Greenland was named by Eric the Red in 985. Why he gave the frozen island that name remains unclear."

He was high on mead? Just a wild guess.

Leash skimmed to the next section, called *Strategic Importance.* This sounded catchy. Maybe the State Department drone had managed to produce one juicy chapter.

"The weather stations in Greenland send out daily reports of crucial value to the North Atlantic theatre. This is a matter of life and death, as German U-boats attack Allied convoys every day. Germans troops, sent from Norway, have tried twice to establish their stations on the eastern coast. This happened at Mackenzie Bay and Sabine Island. Although all known German outposts have been taken out of commission in air strikes, the existence of undiscovered bases remains a possibility. Another soft spot are the cryolite mines in Ivigtut, which are vital in the production of aircraft-grade alu—"

The last words drifted off before Leash's eyes. He fell asleep, face buried in the pages. A woman's face slowly faded into his dream, the image blurry and sepia-toned like an old, silent film. It was a familiar face.

CHAPTER II

THE SKY was ashen like an embalmed corpse. A few orphaned clouds hunched at the horizon, strung across in a wispy trail. The twin propellers of a Gooney Bird whirred with a rolling hum. The plane sailed due north, straight into the grim embrace of the polar night. With each minute the heavens got darker, as if an unseen god of winds was sucking the daylight out of them. Two thousand feet below raged the gray Atlantic, its waves lashed into foamy ropes by a western wind. A flock of seagulls passed by, headed south. The birds eyed the plane curiously, as if surprised to see someone foolish enough to head north.

The cargo hold vibrated with the muffled drone of the engines. With its grimy, ribbed walls, the hold could pass for a belly of a whale. A central aisle split it in half, rows of wooden benches on either side. Three squads of Rangers reclined on the benches, swaddled in blankets and winter parkas, their Tommy guns at their feet. Half of the men slept, their breath oozing out in puffs of vapor. The air reeked of engine oil. A battered old phonograph on the floor played an out-of-place, almost surreal melody: Vivaldi's *Four Seasons*.

Leash sat in the back, gazing at his troop. He had always been puzzled by the big riddle of war. How is it possible that random men, who had never met in peacetime, come to trust each other with their lives in times of war? If they all had met before the war for a beer, how many of them would have even cared for the others' company? A few, maybe. Many would've hated each other outright. Yet here they were, a unit, their fates bound in life and death.

His eyes flitted between the familiar faces. It wasn't often that he got to see the whole gang in a quiet scene like this.

Off to the right sat Rufus. Angular head, red locks, two manic eyes immersed in a pocket Bible. Every few seconds, he nodded with joy and grinned to himself, as if some bloody tale of the Old Testament was right up his alley. Leash was never quite sure if Rufus was pulling off an act or if the man simply wasn't wired-up right.

Next to Rufus sat Gilchrist and Bradley. They were playing a game of chess, the pieces made from wine corks. Both in their twenties, both from Utah, both had the same keen distrust of others. Maybe it comes with the territory if you're raised in Provo.

Across the aisle from them slept Slocombe, the medic. Filthy towel across his eyes, drooling mouth, skin like a cadaver, strands of brown hair glued to the forehead with unwashed sweat. Leash hated his guts. Everyone knew the man was a damn morphinist. Their old medic had been shot two months ago and the best thing HQ could send in way of replacement was this backstreet junkie. Leash sighed. What could he do? Report Slocombe and get a boozehound instead?

Behind Slocombe sat Hitch and Eiffel. Johanna perched on Eiffel's shoulder, a tiny hood pulled over her head. Eiffel fed the falcon chunks of pemmican from a paper bag. His tense stare was on the deck of Tarot cards spread before him. Eiffel looked worried, as if the cards bode ill. Hitch pulled out a small glass jar and offered it to Eiffel.

"Lip balm?"

Eiffel shook his head without looking. Hitch shrugged, dipped into the jar, and smeared the balm across his mouth.

"Don't come crying to me later."

He smacked with satisfaction and glanced over at Johanna.

"Say, isn't your bird gonna croak in Greenland?"

"She'll be fine. She's half polar."

"Half polar? What's the other half? Irish?"

"You're too funny, Hitch."

Eiffel frowned, his eyes on a Tarot card. He cast a nervous glance out the window at the ocean below.

"How cold do you think that water is?" he said.

Hitch eyed Eiffel with amusement. That paranoid look on Eiffel's face was an old acquaintance.

"Forty. Hypothermia in two minutes. Why?"

Eiffel showed Hitch the Tarot card. *A maiden.*

"It's a bad day for Virgos."

Hitch rolled his eyes. *Jesus H. Christ, who made this nutcase a sergeant?*

"What? Don't you believe in fate?" Eiffel said.

"Only the kind dealt by Molly."

Hitch brandished his Bowie knife with the proud look of a father showing off his firstborn. Eiffel glanced at the knife with disgust, as if the faces of the knife's victims stared back at him from the shiny blade.

"Why do you always haul that goddamn jungle knife, anyways? There ain't no jungle in Greenland."

"Not true, Eiffel," Hitch lowered his voice. "Men bring their jungle wherever they go."

Across the aisle from them sat Mopey, a lanky kid not older than twenty. He had a pale, doughy face and skinny arms that looked like they had been made out of putty and stretched out of proportion. A deck of cards in his hand, he turned to Eiffel, his voice squeaky and stuttering.

"Na-na-name a card, Sa-sa-sarge."

"Six of clubs."

Mopey tossed the cards up. When they spread out in a vertical column, he snapped up one card mid-air. The deck fell back neatly into his hand. Mopey showed the card he'd snatched: six of clubs. He sighed.

"Sh-sh-should've stuck out the ma-magic school."

Seated away from the Rangers, May and Ramsey watched all of this with cold, unimpressed eyes. Hitch took notice. Mischief in his eyes, he turned to Mopey.

"Try the queen of hearts."

Mopey tossed the cards up again. Before he managed to do anything - whoosh! Hitch's knife zipped through the air, missing Mopey's hand by an inch, and nailed the queen of hearts to a wooden crate.

"You cra-crazy?!" Mopey leapt toward Hitch. "Nearly cho-cho-chopped my hand off!"

Jerome, a six-foot-five tree trunk of a man, gently held Mopey back.

"Easy, Mopey."

Jerome then leaned toward Hitch, pure threat in his eyes. He leaned so close that Hitch could smell the Red Man chew on his breath.

"Stay away from my brother, 'cause he's the only one I've got."

Jerome and Hitch locked a hard stare for a few tense seconds. Hitch shrugged it off and got up to retrieve his knife.

Seeing this, May shook her head, picked up a thermos, and headed down the aisle. Eiffel leaned toward Hitch once she'd passed by.

"Doesn't a broad on deck bring bad luck?"

"Relax. Only at sea."

Eiffel nodded with relief. He then frowned and looked out the window. The ocean stretched to the horizon.

Leash twirled a pencil. Spread open on his lap lay a sketchbook filled with drawings of sailboats. He gazed out the window. Why is it that a view from a plane always served up this nagging stew of nostalgia? The memories chased one another. His childhood in Philly. The day he struck out on his own. The day he entered Penn State. The day he enlisted. The day he met her. The day they married. The day she up and—

The image of her face lingered before his mind's eye. He touched the empty spot on his finger. The ring hadn't been there for a long year. Donated to the war effort. Probably melted down in some rusty furnace in Pittsburgh. Failed love in the service of liberty. Leash sighed. Why don't they give medals for patriotism borne out of a broken heart?

"May I?"

The female voice gave Leash a jolt. He snapped right out of the memory closet. Hell, you could hear him slam the closet door shut. He looked up, covering his embarrassment with a mask of indifference.

May stood next to him, offering a cup of coffee. Leash eyed the cup with a cold stare.

He fought hard to hold back the "go away" that had made its way to the tip of his tongue. Breaking the flow of memories ranked up there with murder in his personal penal code.

"What's this?" he said.

"An icebreaker. Forgive the pun."

A hesitant pause. Leash took the cup. It took him a few seconds to mumble a reply.

"Sorry about those remarks. It's just—"

"I don't want special treatment, Captain. Just respect. That's special enough."

Leash nodded with an unconvinced look. He wasn't sure if he was agreeing with her or just affirming his original doubts. Out of the corner of his eye, he saw her nervously scratch her neck, just above her necklace. He sneaked a closer look. Now he knew why the oversized corals. A reddish, quarter-sized birthmark peeked out from behind. She kept scratching that spot over and over. Funny, how people draw attention to their secrets when they're trying too hard to hide them.

She pointed toward the Rangers. "A rowdy bunch you got there. You hand-picked them all?"

Leash nodded. He knew full well she was just trying to small-talk him into conciliation, but his vanity got the better of him. He rarely had a chance to give someone a tour of his unit. He pointed to Hitch, who was cleaning his already clean knife.

"That's Hitch. A knife fiend. Half his skills are illegal under the Geneva Convention. That includes his big mouth." Leash lowered his voice. "He got a ten-year sentence for knifing. The Rangers promised him a pardon if he serves this tour."

His eyes turned toward Eiffel.

"Eiffel's paranoid. He's been seeing bad omens ever since a mortar shell hit the ground two feet from him and didn't go off. See his bird? He trained her to track humans."

He moved on to Mopey and Jerome.

"Mopey and Jerome, love-hate brothers from Wisconsin. Can't agree who'll get the family farm. They won't let anything happen to each other, 'cause they'd have no one else to drive crazy."

He pointed to Rufus, immersed in his Bible. "Rufus there trained to be a Pentecostal preacher, then decided that a gun speaks louder than a lectern. God, does he still enjoy a good sermon."

He noticed May wasn't listening. She gazed curiously at the boat drawings in his sketchbook.

"What did *you* do before the war? Design boats?"

"Four years as a civil engineer." He shrugged. "Always wanted to build a boat. Maybe when it's over."

"Got someone to name it after?"

Leash's eyes narrowed to two guarded slits. The small-talk was headed straight for the minefield.

"I need the boat to get away from memories, not cling to them."

"Get away or find a cheap replacement?"

"As a replacement, it's damn effective." Leash's face soured. "Boats don't sail away on their own."

For a few tense moments, they sat still, bearing the burden of the awkward silence. May opened her mouth to say something, but the crackling of the intercom cut her off.

"Captain! Fire signals!"

Leash glanced out the window. They were above Greenland. A circle of yellow dots shimmered near the coastline. He leapt to his feet and yelled.

"Okay, daisies, we're coming up on the LZ!"

The Rangers sprang up from their seats.

"Fire signals?" Hitch put on a surprised face. "No limos?"

Jerome lifted the forty pounds of his M1919 machine gun and kissed its barrel.

"Tango time, Deuce."

The Rangers flung the chute packs over their shoulders and lined up in a file facing the door. Each man checked the chute of the man before him. Someone yanked the cargo door open. A gust of wind whooshed in, snow-flakes whirling. Leash took a deep breath.

Ouch. The air was harsh, as if millions of tiny icicles hung suspended in it.

May stood next to him, ready for a tandem jump.

"Remember: legs together, muscles relaxed," he said.

He could see her irises dilated with fear. She tried hard to hide it. *Too hard.*

"You scared?" he said.

"A bit."

"Save some goose bumps for the Germans."

May smiled feebly.

"Captain, we're on target!" the intercom crackled.

Leash firmed his grip on the chute release. "All right, men! Go!"

His voice thundered down the cargo hold. One by one, the Rangers jumped out.

The snow plain stretched for miles. A few scattered bonfires blazed up, fighting the wind. Inuk, an Inuit in a furry parka, stoked the flames. He was in his thirties, his broad face sanded down by winds. A ten-year-old boy helped him. High above, they heard the hum of a plane. A tiny speck shimmered against the dark sky, trailing a flock of white dots. The dots grew and mushroomed into dozens of parachutes.

"Tell them they're here!" Inuk said.

The boy hurried off. Inuk rushed over to a nearby snow mound and hid behind it. Never hurts to be on the safe side. He watched the parachutes swoop down. *Plop! Plop! Plop!* They landed in the snow one by one, kicking up powdery clouds. The paratroopers promptly buried their chutes, gathered the bags with equipment, and hurried toward the bonfires.

Inuk listened intently: they spoke English. He stepped out of hiding, waved them over and stretched out his hand toward the leader.

"Inuk Jakobsen, Danish Greenland Patrol."
"Captain Leash, U.S. Rangers."
"Follow me, please."
He headed off onto the snow plain.

❋ ❋ ❋

So here it was: Greenland.
When worlds collide . . . Leash couldn't quite remember
where he'd heard those words. But they fit to a T the image of a U.S. commando unit parading through igloos
in the middle of an Arctic wasteland.

The snow crunched under his boots loud and clear. It
felt like tramping on top of a giant glazed donut. Leash
looked around. They marched through the Inuit village,
trying not to draw attention. They sure as hell had drawn
it. The whole village peered at them from inside their
snow homes. Leash could see the fear in the shy eyes.
Their presence here couldn't possibly be a good omen
for the natives. The huskies barked at them, but were
quickly silenced. It all looked strange, almost surreal, as
if everyone played a collective peek-a-boo. The Rangers
pretended they weren't there and the Inuit pretended
not to see them.

"Do they know why we're here?" Leash eyed Inuk.

"They don't care much about the war. What matters
to them are the blizzard season and seal migrations. All
they were told is to watch out for soldiers with a red flag
and a black cross."

"At least they know we're the good guys," Leash
sighed.

"There are no good guys coming to Greenland, Captain," Inuk shook his head. "Just outsiders."

One of the igloos stood apart. As they passed, Leash
looked through the open doorway. A shaman sat inside,
half-hidden behind a curtain of walrus hides. He was an

old, craggy wizard dressed up in claw necklaces and a wolf-skin cap. He gaped at the Rangers with tranced-out eyes, mumbled some incantations, and scattered a fistful of tiny bones in a circle around him.

"What's he doing?" Leash turned to Inuk.

"Dog bones. Protection spell."

Hitch covered his mouth to contain the giggles.

"Against what? Ghosts?" Leash said.

"There's a land in our legends," Inuk said, "*Atshen*, The Land of the Beast. An evil ground where people don't go and animals don't dare."

His tone was somber, almost morose. He pointed in the direction they were headed. "That place is Thule Bay."

The Rangers traded uneasy looks. Hitch shrugged, unfazed. Leash shot Inuk a sideways glance. The man looked damn serious about all this.

The Rangers filed behind Inuk toward the nearby hills. Leash could feel the anxious gaze of the villagers burrowing into his back.

The rugged hill range swept through the plain to the glacier-clad horizon. Inuk and the Rangers stood at the foot of a steep cliff. A talus of ice debris leaned against the cliff wall. Hidden just behind it was the mouth of an ice cave. Leash headed over and played his flashlight around. The cave dropped deep into the bowels of the hill.

"Can we all squeeze in?" Leash said.

Inuk shook his head.

"Two men only. Too narrow."

Leash turned to Hitch. "You and Inuk climb in and let us in from inside. We'll take the gear and cross the hills straight through."

Hitch nodded. Leash patted him on the back. "See you on the other side."

Hitch and Inuk stepped into the cave, climbing axes in hand. The others stood outside, listening. For a few moments, the cave echoed back the clangor of the axes. Soon the noise died down.

"Let's go," Leash said.

The Rangers plodded up the nearby hillside, hauling sleds with equipment.

"Goddamn it, what a rat hole!"

Hitch clenched his jaws. He and Inuk wrestled with a narrow, serpentine passage. It twisted and curled like the bowels of some frozen mastodon. Their flashlights glittered across the blue, crystalline walls; their heavy breaths lingered in vapory swirls. His body bent into a pretzel, Hitch straddled a three-foot-wide crevasse in the floor, trying to get on the other side. Knocked by his boot, a chunk of ice fell down the crevasse. Hitch shone his flashlight straight down. The chunk shimmered for while, then vanished in a bottomless chasm. Hitch's eyes widened in awe.

"Damn it, this drops all the way to China!"

All of a sudden . . . *crack!*

He lost his footing. His left boot began to slide down into the crevasse . . .

"Jesus!"

Inuk dashed over and grabbed him. Not a second too soon. Hitch frantically felt the crevasse wall with his boot. Finally, he secured a footing. Inuk braced himself and lugged him out.

"Thanks," Hitch sighed with deep-felt relief. He wiped his forehead and glanced at his sleeve, surprised. "Amazing, how much you sweat inside a freezer."

The Handie-Talkie crackled. Leash's voice echoed among the walls with pristine clarity.

"How far off are you, Hitch?"

"Half an hour, if we don't bust our bones. It's one nasty hole, sir."

"Report as soon as you see something."

"Copy that, sir."

Hitch shoved the antenna into the radio to turn it off. Inuk turned toward the cave before them. He crouched, squinted, and took an appraising look.

"Look at the cave floor," he said.

"What about it?"

"It's sloping up. We're getting close."

❊ ❊ ❊

Seen from a bird's eye view, Thule Bay looked grandiose, like a giant amphitheater all decked out for a Wagnerian opus. The frozen bay stretched to the east, wrought by frost pressure into badlands of towering ice plates. The hill range in the west clasped the bay in a U-shaped embrace. A string of black specks dotted the ridge: the Rangers.

They stood on a hilltop, panting from effort. Leash wiped the sweat off his forehead and looked downhill, intrigued.

"Looky what we've got here."

A large military base sprawled beneath them. Barracks, radar stations, vehicle shops, and watchtowers clumped together around a grid of access roads, all surrounded by a perimeter fence. Long-necked cranes jutted skyward from the docks area. The bulging globes of fuel silos nestled by the shore. The compound was silent, as if human life had never been a part of it at all. Only gales whistled in the distance.

Leash peered through his binoculars, scanning every inch of the base. No motion. No chimney smoke. No spinning fans. No nothing. A lone German flag hung limply from a mast. The place looked like a still photograph.

"Not a damn soul," Leash said.

He put the binoculars away and looked down. The hillside was smooth and naked; a few scattered moraines provided little cover. Not good. There was no other way to get to the base. Leash signaled Rufus to come over and pointed to May.

"Keep her a hundred feet behind, in case it gets hot. We'll give you a holler once we get a foothold."

Rufus nodded and stepped toward May. Leash raised his hand.

"All right, let's head—"

The crackling of the radio cut him off.

"Too bad you can't see this, sir!"

"Whatcha got, Hitch?"

"Some whopping cavern with animal bones!"

Hitch and Inuk stood inside a big, underground ice cavern, playing their flashlights around. Above their heads, a thousand icicles hung like a phalanx of daggers. Distant drips echoed down the glassy walls. Hitch held his radio tight against his mouth.

"Spooky place, sir."

He shone his flashlight down. The floor was littered with animal bones.

"Looks like a lair of a—"

He flinched, startled. For a brief, scary moment, his flashlight caught the glimpse of a monstrous, beastly snout. Hitch steeled himself and looked closer. Leaning against the cavern wall was a dead polar bear. Its mouth yawned open, frozen in a toothy howl. The carcass was gutted.

The Handie crackled with Leash's voice.

"What is it, Hitch?"

"Looks like a gutted bear. The damn bastard gave me a jolt."

Inuk leaned over to inspect the bear's torn belly. His eyes glinted with anxiety.

"What did this to him?" Hitch said. "A predator?"

Inuk shook his head.

"No animal preys on bears."

"Germans, maybe?"

"If they had found this cave, they'd have secured the entrance."

They gaped at the bear in uneasy silence. Leash's voice cut it short.

"Get moving. We can't lose time."

Inuk and Hitch picked up their gear and moved on.

Behind them, the bear's bulging eyes sank back into darkness.

The cave sloped up. Hitch and Inuk struggled uphill, their cheeks red with effort. All of a sudden Inuk stopped and switched off his flashlight and signaled Hitch to do the same. Thirty feet ahead, a faint patch of light seeped in through a fist-sized hole in the cave wall. They sneaked up and peeked in.

They saw a room-sized dump pit carved in the ice. Rusty oil drums and metal scrap littered the floor. A feeble light shone through an overhead grating.

Inuk's voice dropped to a whisper. "We're under the base." He stretched his hand toward Hitch. "Best of luck."

They shook hands. Inuk gazed up with apprehension, as if they'd landed below a cemetery. "There's some evil around here," he whispered.

"Yeah, a whole SS battalion."

Inuk shook his head, grim-faced. "Not that kind of evil." He wheeled about and vanished into the cave.

Hitch shrugged. He widened the hole with his climbing axe and clambered into the dump pit.

Once inside, he sized up the distance to the overhead grating: seven feet, maybe more. He grabbed an oil drum, set it upright, and climbed atop, trying not to make noise. His eyes were an inch below the grating. He lifted it up with caution and peeked out.

He was at the bottom of a large, industrial hall, its grimy walls made of corrugated metal. German military vehicles hunched in a long row, their engines exposed for repair. A few hanging bulbs swayed gently in the air. The lights were out. Not a soul in sight. Hitch pulled the antenna out of his Handie and whispered into the mike.

"I'm in the vehicle shop. The power's out. No one around."

He pushed the grating up, set it gently on the floor, and climbed out of the pit. Gun at the ready, he crept between the vehicles to the half-open shop door. He peeked out.

Before him was an empty yard. Off to the side loomed a tall, armored entrance gate. Next to it stood a sentry box. A rifle barrel jutted out from inside.

Hitch held his radio tight to his mouth. "I'm on the other side of the gate. There's a sentry box off to the side. I can see his rifle."

He wetted his lips like a cheetah ready for a kill. "I'm going in."

Knife in hand, he sneaked along the yard's perimeter toward the sentry box. When he was only a few steps away, he made a dash for it, grabbed the sentry's rifle and raised his knife . . .

Leash and his troop had climbed down to the foothills. They crouched behind a cluster of ice boulders, peering out at the base before them. About fifty yards away rose the armored entrance gate. It was shut tight.

A tall fence ran around the perimeter, fortified with a dozen watchtowers.

Eiffel readied his falcon for a flight. "Come on, Johanna. See who's in there!"

The bird fluttered off, soared three hundred feet up, and began circling above the base.

Leash scanned the watchtowers through his binoculars. Not a damn soul.

Zzzzzt!

They flinched, startled by a metallic creak. The gate jerked and began to slide open. Eyes narrowed in tension, the Rangers followed its movement. The gate rolled away, revealing the yard behind. Someone stood on the other side, pulling the gate open. The Rangers caught the glimpse of a polar parka. They tightened their grips on their guns. Leash was the first to see the face.

"Easy! It's Hitch."

Hitch stood on the other side of the gate, the sentry's rifle in his hand, a look of confusion on his face. The Rangers jumped out from hiding and rushed toward the gate. Leash drilled his eyes into Hitch.

"Did you get the sentry?"

"Looks like someone else did."

Leash stepped toward the sentry box and peeked in. It was empty. A report book and a pen were still there, untouched. Hitch checked the lock of the sentry's rifle.

"He left a loaded gun."

The Rangers exchange puzzled glances.

A pair of wings fluttered overhead. Johanna returned from the recon flight and perched on Eiffel's shoulder. Eiffel watched the bird closely as it groomed its wing.

"She didn't see anyone," Eiffel said.

A distant mast swayed in the wind with rhythmic, jarring creaks. They sounded like taunts. Mopey scanned the surroundings, fear gathering in his eyes.

"Sir, where di-di-did everyone go? What's go-going on here?"

Ramsey cut him short.

"That's what we're here to find out."

Leash eyed Ramsey. The man looked unfazed by the strange goings-on. Must have been pretty good at putting up a front.

Ramsey spread out a map of the base and pointed to a marked spot.

"We need to get to the ice piles. The labs must be below. I bet that's where they keep the professor."

The Rangers surrounded him, their eyes on the map. Eiffel assessed the lay of the land.

"We'll need to cross the whole damn base to get there!"

Leash scrutinized the map. He pondered something for a moment and pointed to a blocky outline on the outskirts.

"Eiffel, take your squad and get to the power plant. We need to turn the juice back on or we'll freeze our heinies off. If you meet resistance, radio in for help."

He pointed to a large building in the center. "I'll take the rest to headquarters. We'll set up forward command there. Radio check every fifteen minutes."

Leash eyed Eiffel. "Got it?"

Eiffel nodded. He gathered his squad and marched off due west.

Mopey kept peering around with apprehension.

"I don-don-don't like this—"

Jerome gave him a solid pat on the back.

"Chin up, son," Jerome said, his voice peppy and unfazed. He brandished his M1919. "We're going in force, and we're going for blood."

They headed north along a snowbound road.

CHAPTER III

LEASH AND HIS TROOP edged ahead in a combat formation. They peered around with baffled faces. The surroundings looked like the aftermath of a riot: scattered debris, abandoned weapons, deserted vehicles. A frigid wind drifted snow through the base, rousing an orchestra of sinister noises. A half-open door squeaked in the distance, a rusty sign flapped on a chain-link fence with a manic clank. It sounded like devil banging on the timpani. Curlicues of snow fanned off the roofs and fell down in wispy waterfalls. No one was around. The base looked like the last remnant of a civilization that had died eons ago. Hitch furrowed his brow.

"What the hell is this? A mass desertion?"

"May-may-maybe a plague?" Mopey covered his mouth cautiously.

Leash frowned and listened intently.

"Quiet!"

They heard a muffled, rustling noise of soft objects rubbing against each other. In an instant they leveled their Tommy guns and scanned the environs. Leash pointed straight ahead.

"In there!"

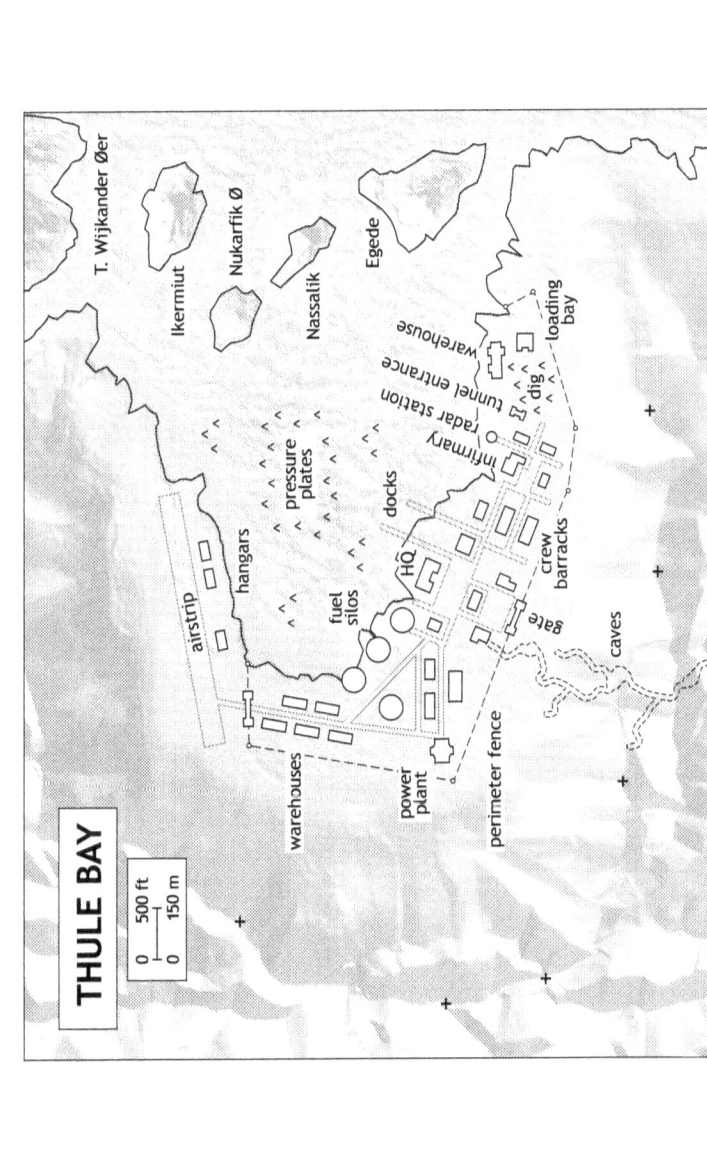

THULE BAY

0 ___ 500 ft
0 ___ 150 m

T. Wijkander Øer

Ikermiut

Nukarfik Ø

Nassalik

Egede

warehouse

loading bay

dig

tunnel entrance

radar station

infirmary

docks

pressure plates

crew barracks

HQ

gate

caves

hangars

fuel silos

airstrip

warehouses

power plant

perimeter fence

About a hundred feet up ahead, a German military van hunched abandoned off the road. Leash peered through his binoculars. Small, vague shapes whirled inside the cabin. His voice dropped to a whisper.

"Bradley, Gilchrist! Get the door!"

The two Rangers crept up to the van's rear door and gripped the handles. The others trained their guns on the van, ready to blast away. Leash gave a signal.

"Now!"

Bradley and Gilchrist yanked the door open . . .

Whoosh!

A fluttering mass gushed out of the van and shot straight up in the air. The Rangers dropped for cover, startled. It was a flock of seagulls. The birds circled above, squawking angrily.

Guns at the ready, Leash and others moved toward the van and peeked in. Inside lay a dead German soldier, his face reduced to pulp by the birds. He held a handgun to his bloody temple. Hitch climbed into the van. He checked the man's sleeve insignia and his wound.

"It's the sentry," Hitch called out to Leash. "He shot himself."

A silver object glinted in the sentry's clenched fist. Hitch pried open the stiff fingers and plucked out the object. He jumped out of the van and showed Leash his find. It was a German belt buckle, inscribed *Gott mit uns.*

"He sure wanted God on his side," Hitch said.

Mopey gaped at the buckle, frightened. "Sir, why-why-why did he shoo-shoot himself?"

No one had an answer. Leash frowned, his face pulled taut in concern. He reached for his Handie.

"Dakota to Blue Seal, Dakota to Blue Seal. Talk to me, Eiffel."

"I can see the power plant," the radio rasped with Eiffel's voice. "We'll try to get close."

"Keep your eyes open. Seems like something—" Leash searched for the right word, "*bad* happened here."

"What do you mean, sir?"

"I wish I knew."

"Roger, sir."

Leash turned his radio off. "Let's get moving."

They started down the access road. Leash slammed the van's door shut. The mangled face of the sentry vanished in the dark.

Leash and his troop crouched hidden behind an abandoned half-track. Before them was a large yard, littered with debris. On the other side loomed an imposing, two-story building. Hitch scanned it through his binoculars: broken windows gaped open, a torn German flag hung limply above the entrance. The sign by the door read *Kommendantur.*

"Headquarters," Hitch said. "Looks clean."

The watcher peered out through a small window in the pitch-black basement of the HQ building. He couldn't see the Rangers directly, but he could make out some motion across the yard. Vague shadows moved there, and tiny crumbs of snow slid off vehicles, as if someone had bumped into them. The eyes of the watcher flitted from vehicle to vehicle, trying to identify the intruder.

On the other side of the yard, Leash signaled the Rangers.

"All right. We're going in."

Mopey raised his head and—

Bang!

A lone shot echoed throughout the yard. The bullet zinged off the half-track with a cascade of sparks, missing Mopey's head by an inch.

"Cover!" Leash yelled.

The Rangers hugged the ground. Jerome downed his brother out of harm's way.

"Sir, he almost licked Mopey!"

A few more shots rang out. The bullets hammered the half-track in a clanging staccato. Hitch spied a nearby truck. He dash-rolled over and dived underneath. From there he scanned the yard through his binoculars.

There. He saw it. A faint wisp of smoke lingered near one of the basement windows.

"Shooter in a rabbit hole!" Hitch yelled. "Basement window, second left!"

"How many?!" Leash yelled back.

"Can't tell, sir!"

Hitch's eyes swept the yard between them and the building. Nothing but flat, open space.

"He got us nailed good, sir! Can't get no cover!"

Leash peered around, eyes narrowed to tense slits. He spied a massive snowplow parked in a nearby garage. A sudden idea flashed in his eyes.

"Cover me!"

He bolted toward the snowplow.

The watcher in the basement saw a rapid motion in the yard. His gun cracked again.

The Rangers blasted away at the basement. The bullet hits sizzled around the window like grease in a frying pan. The shooter fell silent.

Leash climbed into the plow's cabin and pulled the starter lever. The engine gasped and died. Leash tried again. The gasp grew louder. Leash tried one more time.

The engine choked, spat out globs of jelled oil, and started. Leash revved it up hard and threw it into gear.

The snowplow shot out of the garage like a longhorn from a corral. It pulled into the yard, headed for the HQ building. The shooter in the basement let loose a raking salvo into the plow. Bullets zinged off the blade; sparks flew left and right. The windshield took a hit and shattered to pieces. Leash ducked for cover but he held the course steady. The machine chugged along toward the HQ building, piling up snow before the blade.

The shooter peered out the basement window. It was getting tight. The snowplow charged on; the snow pile loomed larger every second.

Leash jammed on the gas. The engine roared and sped up. The snow pile was only yards away from the building, about to pound into the wall.

Hitch sneered with glee. "Big mama's coming to hug you, Fritz!"

Whomp!

The plow hit the building head on, the impact cushioned by the snow pile. The engine howled, stalled against the building. An avalanche of snow gushed in through the basement window, burying everything inside.

All of a sudden the door of the HQ building slammed open. A German soldier in his twenties bolted out. He was dirty and emaciated, his white *Wehrmacht* parka torn to rags. With his deranged eyes he looked like a hermit tormented by demons. Gun in hand, he darted out onto the yard. He stopped in the center and blasted a vicious salvo . . . straight down *into the snow!*

"*Mich wirst Du nicht kriegen, Du verdammtes Ungeheuer!*" he screamed his lungs out.

Leash gestured his men. "Hold your fire!"

He didn't have to say anything. The Rangers had already stopped firing. Eyes wide in bewilderment, they gaped at the lunatic in the yard.

"What the hell is he doing?" Hitch said.

The German soldier kept firing into the snow around him. Leash couldn't make any sense out of it. The man must have lost all sanity in the basement.

The German's gun clanked empty. He hurled it away, dropped down, and curled up in a fetal position.

Leash knew he had to move quick. He waved a signal. Guns drawn, the Rangers sprang out of hiding and stormed the building. Bradley and Gilchrist grabbed the German. He fought tooth and claw, but was overpowered. When he saw who had captured him, he slumped with resignation.

The Rangers fanned out inside the building to search it. The two floors inside were filled with offices, all in disarray: paperwork scattered on the floor, broken furniture. The lights were out. No one was there.

Leash entered the building. Jerome trotted over with a report.

"All rooms clear, sir! We found a map room, big enough for a command center!"

"Secure all floors!" Leash said. "Set up trip wires and post guards outside! Two hour shifts!"

The Rangers hurried off.

Leash turned on his radio. "Rufus, come on over. We've found ourselves a home."

Knife in hand, Hitch sneaked downstairs into the basement where the German had made his hideout. He played his flashlight around and waded through the pile of snow that had poured in through the window. He tripped over something rigid buried in the snow.

"Goddamn it!"

He leaned over to shove the snow aside and examine the object. A grimace of disgust twisted his face.

Hitch emerged from the basement with a morose look. Leash eyed him curiously.

"What d'ya find?"

"His pal. Dead for days." He paused. "Half-eaten."

Bradley and Gilchrist led their prisoner into the building. Hitch watched him with pity. The German dragged his feet, too weak to support his body. The madness in his eyes gave way to torpor.

"Seems like he got stuck with a corpse and hunger got the better of him," Hitch said.

Leash looked out a window to survey the surroundings. "Strange."

"Why?" Hitch said. "If I were stuck for days, I'd do the same thing."

"That's not what I meant." Leash shook his head. "What's strange is that a man goes cannibal even though he's got a pantry right before his nose."

Hitch followed Leash's gaze. Just across the yard, two hundred feet from the HQ building, stood a warehouse: its gate open, its shelves stocked with canned food.

"What held him back?" Hitch said.

"Fear?"

Gilchrist approached Leash.

"We found his papers, sir."

He handed Leash a German soldier's card. Leash read the hand-written name. "Klaus Ulrich Krause, private, born in *Gel*—" he strained to read the writing, "*Gel-sen-kirch-en.*"

Leash saw Rufus escorting May into the building.

"How's your German?" Leash turned toward her.

"Why?"

"Think you can get him to talk?" Leash pointed to Krause.

"I can try."

"Ask him what the hell he was shooting at."

They approached Krause. May addressed him.

"Wieso haben Sie geschossen?"

Krause's voice was quiet and trembling.

"Ich dachte dass es er war."

"He thought it was *him*," May said.

Leash and Hitch traded puzzled looks.

"Him? Who's *him?"*

Krause's eyes widened with fear, as he peered around.

"Das Gespenst! Das Ungeheuer!"

"What's he saying?" Leash turned to May.

"The ghost. The monster," she said.

"What ghost?" Leash looked at Krause, baffled.

Krause swept his arm and pointed all around.

"You can't see him, but he's everywhere!" he said in accented English. His voice dropped to a paranoid whisper. "He's hiding!"

He grabbed Leash's hand, his eyes dilated with delirium. "You must leave here! This base is alive! You hear me?! *Alive!"*

Leash freed himself from Krause's grip. He turned to the medic.

"Get working on him, Slocombe. Perhaps he'll come to and talk sense."

Slocombe and two Rangers led Krause off. Hitch sighed and shook his head with pity.

"I think he lost it, sir," he said. "Maybe the polar night drove them all bonkers, so they knocked each other off."

Leash fixed May with a questioning stare.

"You know what he was talking about?"

Her gaze fled away. "No."

She whirled and headed off. Hitch followed her with suspicious eyes.

"Sir, I get this feeling she knows something we don't."

Leash and the Rangers stepped into the map room and looked around. The room was painted a sickly green. Broken chairs lay strewn about the floor. German war maps of the Northern Atlantic plastered the walls; a long conference table stretched in the center. A six-foot wide German eagle hung above it, staring down at the Rangers with evil eyes.

"Let's set up camp here—"

Crash!

A noise of shattered glass cut Leash off. The Rangers whirled around, guns trained. On the floor by the wall they saw a framed photo of Hitler, its glass smashed to pieces. Above it stood Jerome, holding out the butt of his rifle. He smiled apologetically.

"Sorry. Couldn't resist."

The Rangers sighed and lowered their guns.

"All right, men," Leash said, "I want the camp set up in half an hour." He nudged a broken chair with his foot. "And clean up this mess."

The Rangers rushed to unpack their gear; a few began to pick up the debris. Jerome rubbed his hands to warm up.

"Can't believe the Krauts left the heating off," he said. "This ain't *gemütlich*. Damn, I'd give my arm for a hot shower."

"Jerome," Leash said, "if you gave your arm, how would you do the washing?"

The troop chuckled. Hitch entered the room clutching a pile of goodies: praline boxes, chocolate bars, and a leather box marked with a German eagle.

"From *Wehrmacht* with love."

He tossed the treats to the Rangers like Santa Claus dispensing presents. The men snatched them eagerly.

"Hey, where did you get all of this?" Rufus gulped a praline.

"Officers' club. Stocked like The Ritz."

Rufus noticed a Cuban cigar in Hitch's mouth.

"Thought you quit smoking."

"I did. I'm just trying to find out if I can do it again."

Hitch opened the leather box and whistled. From inside he pulled out an Iron Cross. He rubbed it clean against his parka, hung it on his chest, and clicked his heels at attention, mocking a German officer.

"*Herr General* Hitch reporting to score with Eva Braun!"

The Rangers hee-hawed.

❉ ❉ ❉

The snow-swept access road wound its way west. Debris lay scattered about; a few abandoned vehicles huddled at the roadside. Eiffel and his squad skulked ahead, Thompsons at the ready. Surrounding them was a ghost town. Somewhere nearby, a half-open door creaked ominously.

Wham!

The door slammed shut. The Rangers jerked and trained their guns that way. No one was there, just the wind. Kaminski, a skinny youngster with pockmarked cheeks, looked around fearfully. The gaping holes of broken windows stared back at him like giant, dark eyes.

"Sir, what if someone's watching us?" he said.

"Shut the hell up!" Eiffel said. "I'm all spooked up as it is."

He signaled his men to stop.

About three hundred feet away up ahead towered the smokestack of a squat, industrial structure.

"Cover!" Eiffel said.

The men hid behind the vehicles. Eiffel peered at the structure through his binoculars. The entrance stood open, revealing a shadowy, industrial interior. Nothing moved inside. Eiffel readied Johanna for a flight.

"See who's home, girl."

The bird flew off and swooped down into the power plant's entrance. Eiffel pulled the antenna out of his Handie and whispered into the mike.

"Sir, we're at the power plant."

The radio crackled with Leash's reply.

"Seen anyone?"

"Looks clear so far."

"Be careful, Eiffel. From what we've seen, they might have all gone nuts and bumped each other off."

Hearing this, Eiffel's men traded puzzled glances.

"All gone nuts, sir?" Eiffel said.

"You heard me. Secure the plant and get working on the juice," Leash said, "We'll croak without heat."

"Roger that, sir."

Eiffel turned off the radio. Johanna returned from the power plant, landed on Eiffel's shoulder, and began to groom her wing with awkward, jerky movements. Kaminski watched the bird with burning eyes.

"What's she saying, Sarge?"

"She saw someone. But . . ."

"But what, Sarge?"

"I don't know. I think she's confused."

Eiffel signaled his men with fingers held up in a V.

"Let's move!"

Guns ready, the squad leapt out from hiding, split into two teams, and stormed the power plant from two sides.

Once inside, they scanned the murky surroundings: hallways, walkways, a battery of valves and control panels. Piping webbed its way around every nook and cranny. The Rangers listened attentively. Nothing but dead silence. Off to the side, Eiffel spied a door labeled *Kontrolstelle*. He pointed it out to the others. Johanna, perched on his shoulder, twitched nervously. Eiffel slid the tiny hood over the bird's eyes.

"Easy, girl," he whispered.

Guns leveled, they sneaked up toward the door and burst in. The control room was about forty feet long, its corners far enough to vanish completely in darkness. Switch panels and consoles lined the walls. Off to the side stood a small table surrounded by four chairs. Kaminski tiptoed toward the table and glanced at what was on it. Coffee cups, a box of biscuits, cigarettes, an ashtray. A hand of cards lay face-down in front of each chair. In the center bulged a pile of money. *Reichsmarks.* Kaminski leaned over and whistled.

"Five-card draw. Nice pot." He checked the hand closest to him and frowned. "Strange. Someone left a full house."

Plonk!

A tiny, hard object fell into the ashtray. Kaminski picked it up. It was a red, frozen chunk that looked like strawberry ice cream. Kaminski frowned and took a whiff.

"Ugh," he grimaced. The frozen chunk had a foul, organic odor. The warmth of his hand began to melt it. It turned to blood, streaked across his hand, and dripped onto the floor. Kaminski frowned, perplexed. He looked up at the ceiling above the table. His eyes bugged out; his face stiffened with dread.

"Sarge . . ."

Eiffel looked at him and followed his gaze up. He aimed his flashlight at the ceiling.

Kaminski's voice quivered with fear. "Christ, what happened here?"

All Rangers now looked up at the ceiling, their eyes open wide in horror. Eiffel reached for his radio. His tone was grim.

"Sir, we found a dozen dead Germans. I don't think they killed each other. I . . ." He struggled to find the right words. "I don't think what killed them was even human."

"How do you know?" Leash said.

Eiffel gulped to clear the clump of dread growing in his throat.

"Because I've never seen an SS squad glued to the ceiling with frozen blood."

A morbid sight loomed above the Rangers. A dozen dead SS men hung face down, backs stuck to the ceiling in big splotches of frozen blood. Their bodies were twisted, their limbs bent at strange angles, like figurines in a medieval Dance of the Dead. Open mouths and deep wounds gave witness to their agony.

CHAPTER IV

LEASH LOOKED AROUND the map room. A few lanterns lit the walls with a dancing, orange glow. A few men were unpacking their gear; others gobbled down corned beef heated over gas burners. The room reeked of propane. This smell would sure ruin a dinner in a suburban kitchen. Here, in the middle of a frozen wasteland, it was quite an appetizer. Leash watched the faces of his men. The meal had raised the spirits.

"Hey, Rufus, what's the difference between a Nazi grunt and a Nazi general?" Jerome said, gulping down his ration.

"You tell me, Jerome."

Jerome pointed to a neat row of notches carved on his gun's butt. "A quarter inch on a Tommy."

"Get outta here," Rufus waved him off. "God, I never thought I'd miss Guadalcanal," he sighed. "I'd rather have the mosquitoes than the ice up my nose."

"You sure about this?" Hitch said. "Remember how we had to chase the leeches off your heinie with hot smokes?"

The Rangers guffawed.

Leash didn't share in the fun. Some dark premonition had taken root in the back of his mind and was gnawing at him without mercy. *Damn it.* No matter how many missions you chalk up, that strange unease follows you like a shadow, just itching to take control.

He took a deep breath to shake off the feeling and looked around the room. Ramsey and May stood apart from the Rangers, heads leaned over in a conspiratorial whisper. Leash watched them for a moment. Should he bother asking?

He crossed the room. May and Ramsey raised their heads and fell silent as soon as he got close.

"Eiffel found a German squad in the power plant," Leash opened. "All dead."

Ramsey and May traded quick looks.

"Sir, I need to know what happened here," Leash eyed Ramsey.

"I'm afraid I can't give you any more detail right now, Captain."

"Sir, with all due respect—"

Ramsey's stare hardened.

"Captain, your orders are to seize the labs and get us there in one piece," he said. His voice was loud and clear. Leash knew full well it was meant to be heard by others. "This mission remains under my command and I will decide *when* and *if* to give you information."

The room fell silent. Leash and Ramsey glared at each other in tense silence. The Rangers gaped at them they way boys in a schoolyard watch an impending fight.

Leash weighed his options. He had none. Better to give up sooner than to let the stupid scene drag out.

He turned toward the Rangers.

"What's this, a peep show?! Get moving! We gotta set up camp before our fannies freeze solid!"

The Rangers promptly returned to their tasks.

Leash strutted out of the room. He ambled down a hallway, jaws clenched with indignation. He needed a few minutes alone. No way they're going to see him nurse his pride in public.

He glanced over into the radio room. Julius, a pudgy radio operator with headphones on, sat before a boxy radio set. The radio's backlit panel flickered on and off. Julius tweaked the knobs, frustration in his eyes.

Leash stepped in. "What's the holdup here, Julius?" he said. "We're ten minutes past contact time!"

"The power keeps breaking off, sir. Seems like the gear got busted during the drop."

"Get it fixed, then!"

Leash headed off. Julius grabbed a screwdriver and began to disassemble the radio.

Outside the HQ building a few Rangers stretched a web of trip wires around the building. Gilchrist and Bradley crouched by one of the wires, empty food cans in their hands. Gilchrist dropped a few small stones into the can.

"Think it will work?" Bradley said.

Gilchrist closed the lid, hung the can on the trip wire, and shook it to test the effect. The stones inside the can rattled out loud. Gilchrist nodded.

"Works every time."

Hitch was studying the base map in the map room. Out of the corner of his eye, he saw May approach him. He glanced at her. She gave off an air of nonchalance.

"Couldn't help seeing the captain's name on his patch," she said in a casual tone.

Hitch eyed her curiously. Her tone was *too* casual.

"Plutarch?" he said.

"Kind of a strange name, isn't it?"

"Well, there's a story behind it. See, his parents couldn't decide on a name. So they went to a public library, picked a random aisle. His mother pointed to a random book. And there it was, black on white. *Plutarch.*" Hitch lowered his voice. "But I wouldn't bring this up with the captain, Miss."

"Why?"

Hitch looked around to check that no one was listening and leaned toward her.

"See . . . His mother wanted a better life. Glamour, fancy dresses, you know. She found a rich guy and left the captain when he was ten." Hitch paused. "He's never forgotten."

May didn't reply. Hitch could see it in her face. The story had touched something inside her.

"You didn't hear it from me, Miss," he said.

May nodded.

Eiffel and his men worked a console in the power plant's control room. The housing was pulled open, its electric guts exposed. A Ranger tech welded together wires, sparks streaking across the room. The sour smell of molten metal spread around. The tech wiped the sweat off his forehead and tugged on the welded wires.

"Should hold solid, sir."

Eiffel turned on his Handie.

"We've got it, sir," he said, "Power plant coming on line."

Leash's voice rasped through the radio.

"Not a minute too soon. We're a breath away from winter sleep."

Eiffel signaled the tech. The tech threw a switch. A mighty crescendo rumbled from the deep bowels of the power plant. The generator was kicking in.

Leash entered the map room. The overhead bulbs were on. The Rangers thronged around electric heaters, rubbing their hands. The filaments glowed a cozy red through the heater grills. Leash switched on his radio.

"Praise the Lord, Eiffel. Warm like mama's oven. Get back when you're done."

"Copy that, sir."

Leash turned his radio off. Out of the corner of his eye, he saw May across the room. She sat alone at a table, a framed photo in her hands. She was watching him closely. Leash glanced over. Her eyes quickly fled away. Leash hesitated. Should he?

He walked over.

She watched him out of the corner of her eye—he could tell. As soon as he got close, she scratched her birthmark in a quick, nervous reaction. Leash took notice. She was getting self-conscious around him. The ice queen in training wasn't all ice yet.

"Edgy fella, that Ramsey," he said.

It took May a moment to respond. "You could stand to calm down yourself."

"Easy for you to say. Not everyone can watch the war from an ivory tower."

"What exactly do you mean?" She fixed him with a cold stare.

"We put our lives on the line and all you and Ramsey do is whisper behind our backs and risk nothing."

"You think this is a joyride for me? It's the first time I'm on a mission like this!" Her voice dropped to a hissing whisper. "You're sure it isn't about something else?"

Leash's guards went up in a jiffy. "Like what?"

"I'm not blind. You act like someone who's been hurt so bad he now always has to fire the first shot. Especially at a woman."

Leash stood mute, like a chastised preschooler. *Damn.* It always hits you like a thunderbolt to find that you're transparent to everyone but yourself.

"For your information," May continued, "I risk as much as you do." She pointed to the framed photo of the elderly man she held in her hands.

"This is the professor held by the Germans." She paused. "He's my father."

She walked off clutching the photo. Leash gaped at her back, dumbfounded. Her last three words echoed through his cranium before they fully registered.

Julius leaned over the gear in the radio room. The casing was pulled off. Screwdriver in hand, he inspected the vacuum tubes. The pilot lights kept flickering on and off.

All of a sudden they all went dead. The overhead light went out, too. Julius frowned and peeked out into the hallway. The lights outside were still on.

He turned on his flashlight and swept the beam around the room. On the wall behind the radio, he spied the power line. He traced it with his flashlight. It ran up to the overhead bulb and exited the room near the door frame. Julius stepped out and marched down the hallway, his eyes on the power line hanging on the wall. It turned a corner and dropped down along a stairway leading to the basement. Julius climbed downstairs, his flashlight on the power line.

The basement was dim and dingy. A few piles of coal leaned against the walls. The air reeked of old potatoes. The power line terminated inside a fuse box, its casing pulled open. One of the fuse sockets was empty. A screw-in fuse lay on the floor beneath. Julius frowned, picked it up, and screwed it back in.

A faint noise came from the shadows behind the coal pile. Julius drew his .45.

"Who's there?!"

No reply. Julius squinted, his eyes trying to pierce the darkness. He spied a small, red point glowing on the floor near a coal pile. He aimed his flashlight that way and tiptoed over. It was a cigarette butt, still burning. He picked it up and checked the brand. *Winston.*

Out of the corner of his eye, Julius noticed a dark silhouette lurking inside a nearby niche. He spun around. A second too late. Someone's right hook knocked him off his feet. His flashlight hit the floor and went out. He heard a clatter of footsteps zipping upstairs.

"Stop or I'll shoot!"

What a bluff that was. Julius couldn't find his flashlight, much less aim his pistol. He scoured the floor in haste . . . *There.* His flashlight. He flicked it on and leveled his pistol. The man was gone. Julius sprinted off in pursuit. When he reached the first landing, he saw the shadow of the fleeing man thirty feet ahead.

"Freeze!"

The man kept running. Julius let loose a round. The man veered off into a cross hallway, the bullet missing him by an inch. Julius dashed toward the hallway junction. He caught a glimpse of the man vanishing at the far end. Julius gave chase, his boots thundering on the floor.

He reached the end of the hallway and stopped in his tracks. His eyes widened in surprise. Before him was the door to the map room. There was no other way out. The Rangers were coming in and out. Pistol in his hand, Julius stepped in and ran his suspicious stare across the assembled faces.

Hitch eyed him curiously. "Something wrong, Julius?" he said.

"Someone messed with the fuse box! I saw him run in here!"

Hitch look around, puzzled. "You're saying it was one of us?"

"I . . . don't know."

"Did you see his face?"

Julius shook his head and lowered his pistol, resigned. Hitch walked up to him and gave him a pat on the back.

"Kinda early for the ghost hour, eh? Normally, the show starts at midnight."

The Rangers guffawed. Julius bit his lip and backed out of the room.

Gilchrist and Bradley stood guard outside the building. They shared a smoke, their breath hovering around in big, lazy swirls. Gilchrist pulled a tiny music box from his pocket and opened it. It played a sweet lullaby. Gilchrist's face lit up with a misty smile.

"You like it? A gift from my girl."

Bradley didn't ever bother to look. His jaw was so stiff from the cold that his voice barely made it through his lips.

"Ever been in a cold this bad?" he said.

"Makes winter in Utah look like Palm Beach."

"No kidding."

Bradley slapped his hands against his body to warm up. "I gotta move or my guts will turn to ice cubes. I'll do the round on the other side. You coming?"

"I ain't moving an inch."

"All right. Gimme one more."

Bradley reached for the smoke, took a draw, and handed it back to Gilchrist.

"Back in five."

He flung his Tommy gun over his shoulder and vanished behind the corner. Gilchrist wedged the cigarette into his mouth. He pulled out his music box and nudged open the lid. The box broke into a gentle tune. Gilchrist smiled with delight.

Leash scanned the map room. The camp was almost set up. Some Rangers were finishing the cleanup; others lay on the floor, swaddled in fleece blankets. May and Ramsey sat at a table, away from others. They leaned over a map of the base and whispered to each other, *sub rosa.* Leash clenched his teeth. God, how he hated all of this hugger-mugger. But there was nothing he could do except play along. He sighed and stepped out.

He marched down the hallway and glanced over into Krause's room. Slocombe was inside, leaning over a desk. He noticed Leash and quickly leapt to his feet, his back to the desk, as if hiding something. Leash stepped in and approached Slocombe. The medic was sweating like a shower, a sheepish grin on his lips. Leash pushed him aside and glanced at the desk. Morphine.

"It's . . . for him," Slocombe pointed to Krause.

Slocombe's tone couldn't possibly be less convincing. Leash sighed. He'd let it slide. The prospect of making a scene simply made him tired. He glanced over toward Krause. The German slept on a bunk bed, curled up like a baby. All that was missing was a thumb in his mouth. That he couldn't do. His arms were tied behind his back.

"How is he?" Leash said.

"Gave him some chow and anodyne," Slocombe said. "What he needs is a day of sleep. Otherwise he'll just keep talking balon—"

Krause's body arched out in a sudden muscle spasm. He clenched his fists, his chest straining to breathe. Leash and Slocombe rushed over and held Krause down.

"Epilepsy?" Leash said.

Slocombe shook his head.

"He's been kicking around like this since he fell asleep. Must be having nightmares."

The spasm eased off. Krause slumped back.

All of a sudden, his eyes popped open. His suspicious gaze flitted between Leash and Slocombe, as if he wasn't sure if this was a dream or reality.

Hitch showed up at the door clutching of a bundle of wooden debris.

"The map room's all clean, sir."

Krause glanced toward Hitch. His eyes bugged out in mortal fear. He screamed at the top of his lungs, leapt off the bed, and hid in a far corner, quivering, as if scared of an unseen danger. Leash and Slocombe rushed to contain him. Krause fought them tooth and nail, his frightened eyes on the debris in Hitch's hands.

Leash took notice.

"Get the hell out of here, Hitch!" he yelled. "You're giving him the shakes!"

Hitch stood at the door, baffled. "What did I do?"

"I don't know! Just get out!"

Hitch stepped out of the room, dropping a broken chair leg. Slocombe managed to grab a syringe with tranquilizer. He jabbed it into Krause's arm and pushed the piston all the way in. Krause gasped, and slumped on the floor with eyes closed.

Leash and Slocombe dragged him back onto the bed. Krause was now sound asleep, his chest rising and falling in a gentle rhythm. Leash ambled to the door and leaned down to pick up the piece of wood Hitch had dropped. He examined it. Just a broken chair leg.

"What was that all about?" Slocombe said.

"Beats me." Leash tossed the leg into the hallway. "Let me know when he comes to."

"Will do, sir."

Gilchrist stood alone outside the building. He drew on the cigarette all the way to the last inch. No way he was going to waste a perfectly good stub.

The cans on the trip wire rattled quietly. Gilchrist stiffened, listening. The cans rattled again. He leveled his Thompson, tiptoed over to the corner of the building, and peeked out. No one was there.

"Bradley?"

There was no response. Instead, Gilchrist heard more rattling. It came from a dark, narrow alleyway between nearby buildings. Gilchrist peered that way, trying to penetrate the darkness.

"Bradley? Is that you?"

Again, no reply. Gun at the ready, Gilchrist sneaked up toward the alleyway and stepped in. He inched forward, feeling his way in between the shadows.

Whoosh!

Something scurried away from under his feet with a loud squeak. Gilchrist trained his gun that way. He sighed with relief. It was a polar fox. The animal glared at him with red, buttony eyes. Gilchrist put on a coy smile and stretched his hand toward the fox to woo it.

"Come here, sweetie. Daddy's got a treat for you."

The fox gazed at him for a moment, then swiveled its head and stared toward the other end of the alleyway. Its eyes narrowed down to wary slits. The animal bared its teeth, growled, backed off slowly and then bolted off. Gilchrist followed the fox's gaze. He froze in surprise.

A seven-foot tall figure stood at the end of the alley, facing Gilchrist. The figure wore a German steel helmet and a ragged trench coat, its tails fluttering in the wind. The helmet tilted down, hiding the face. Gilchrist couldn't make out the details; all he could see was a dark silhouette. The figure stood still for a few moments, seemingly eying Gilchrist. Then it slowly started toward him with a strange, mechanical gait. Each step yielded a metallic creak. Gilchrist furrowed his brow. Was the man a cripple with prostheses? Who the hell knew. No way Gilchrist was going to take any chances. He cocked his gun and trained it at the figure.

"Stop right there, Fritz."

The figure marched toward Gilchrist, unfazed.

"I said *stop!*"

The figure marched on.

Gilchrist wavered, his finger tight on the trigger. Perhaps there was some explanation for all this. Maybe the man was deaf? Or couldn't speak English? *Hell no.* Gilchrist knew damn well something was all wrong here.

A sudden gust of wind blew the figure's coat up. Gilchrist's eyes bugged out in dread.

Striding toward him was a ghost. There was no human body under the trench coat. The coat and the helmet rested on a skeleton made of a big machine gun tripod. The tripod marched on its own, like a possessed puppet. Gilchrist batted his eyelashes.

"Jesus Christ—"

He couldn't hold back anymore. He pumped a long burst right into the figure, shells spraying. The bullets tore into the trench coat like a wheat shredder, till points of light shone all the way through. The ghost marched on. It was now only a few steps away. Gilchrist ceased firing. He gaped at the figure in wide-eyed awe.

"In God's name, what *are* you?!"

His knees went groggy. Shivers ran down his spine; adrenaline flooded his veins. He stood still, hypnotized by a sight he couldn't comprehend.

The figure halted two feet away from him. Slowly, the helmet tilted up, revealing . . . *nothing.* There was no face under the steel helmet, just a dark void. Gilchrist could sense it: the void stared back at him. In the last spasm of sanity, he pulled the trigger one more time.

In vain.

His gun flew out of his hands, yanked out by an unseen force. It arced through the air and landed in the snow yards away.

Gilchrist's eyes opened wide . . .

The distant gunfire stirred up the map room like a beehive. The Rangers leapt to their feet, feeling around for guns. Leash raised his hands.

"Quiet!"

The Rangers froze and listened. The gunshots echoed down the hallways.

"Northwest corner!" Hitch yelled. "It's Gilchrist!"

The Rangers darted out of the room.

Guns drawn, they rushed toward the back of the building and scanned the surroundings. The base stood dark and silent. Only Arctic gales howled in the distance. Hitch spied fresh footprints in the snow and crouched to examine them.

"They've been pacing around here!"

"Search the grounds!" Leash said.

The Rangers dispersed. Leash leaned over to scour the snow. He spied something. From amid the footprints, he picked up a cigarette butt. It was still alight.

Out of a corner of his eyes, he noticed someone lunging from behind a corner. Leash leapt to his feet, his .45 ready . . .

He lowered his pistol. It was Bradley, eyes wide open with anxiety.

"Sir, what happened? I heard shots!"

"Where were you?"

"Doing a round on the other side." Bradley looked around with apprehension. "Where's Gilchrist?"

"That's what I want to know."

Hitch emerged from a dark alleyway between buildings, unease on his face, a Tommy gun in his hands.

"We found his gun, sir."

Leash took it from Hitch's hands and checked the clip. Empty.

"What about Gilchrist?"

Hitch shook his head and bit his lip. He stalled, unsure how to phrase the answer.

"I . . . I think he's . . . *gone*, sir."

"What you mean, *gone?*"

"You better see it for yourself, sir."

Hitch led Leash and Bradley into the alleyway.

A group of Rangers stood at the other end, gaping at the ground. Leash followed their gaze. A lone trail of footprints dotted the snow; a string of blood splotches ran alongside. The trail led out of the alleyway and into an open plain.

Leash's gaze followed the tracks. His eyes widened in surprise. The footprints ended abruptly, smack dab in the middle of the plain. There was no trace of Gilchrist. No trace of anyone else.

Leash's face tensed up. He took a deep breath to cool his mind down. The scene before him could easily pass for a bad dream. Except there was no denying his own senses. Gilchrist had vanished off the face of the Earth.

Hitch crouched to scrutinize the footprints.

"Big paces. He must've been running away."

Mopey peered around. His wide eyes had the terrified look of a deer surrounded by hunters.

"Ru-ru-running from what?"

No one offered a reply.

Mopey kept peering around. "Ca-ca-captain, I'm scared."

"You're not alone, Mopey," Bradley said.

Leash scanned the environs with a grim stare. "Alone? I get the feeling we're not alone here."

He caught a glimpse of something in the snow. Behind the corner of a nearby building lay a pile of what looked like torn rags. Leash headed over and picked it up. It was a German trench coat, shredded by bullet holes. The Rangers gaped at it, their brows furrowed in a tense suspicion.

Hitch was the first to blurt it out loud.

"The Kraut! The Kraut did it!"

That's all the goading they needed. They dashed back into the HQ building, boots thundering down the hallways.

They burst into Krause's room. Krause's bunk was empty.

"He got out!" Jerome yelled.

Hitch signaled the others.

"Search the building! The bastard might still be around!"

The Rangers scattered into the hallways.

His M1919 leveled, Jerome charged down a narrow corridor. Halfway down, he stopped in his tracks. A small, metallic object glinted on the floor. He picked it up. It was a German dog tag stamped with the name *Krause*. Jerome polished it against his parka, his face scrunched up in a sinister scowl.

"Christmas gift for your folks, Fritz."

He glanced off to the side. Right next to him was a storage closet, its door closed. Jerome squinted with suspicion. A faint shadow moved in the crack under the door.

Jerome yanked the door open and shoved his gun right in.

"I got him!"

The others raced over and peeked into the closet.

Private Krause huddled in a dark corner, shaking like a newborn pup, his arms behind his back. He eyed the Rangers with abject fear. Hitch gripped him by the shoulders.

"What did you do to Gilchrist, you son of a bitch?!"

Jerome trained his gun at Krause's forehead, teeth clenched. "I say we bump him off right here."

At that moment Leash stepped in and shoved Jerome's gun away from Krause.

"Leave him alone! He's scared out of his mind!"

He took Krause by his elbow and helped him up. Krause wobbled on his shaky knees. Hitch glared at the German with a lethal stare.

"Sir, what if he did Gilchrist in?!"

Leash eyed his men. Vengeance burned in their eyes; they were a step away from a lynch mob. Without a word, Leash spun Krause around.

"How?"

Krause's arms were still tied behind his back. Leash fixed his troop with a hard stare. They lowered their guns, faces hung in shame.

"Tell Slocombe to take care of him," Leash said.

One of the Rangers led Krause off.

Leash's eyes flooded with anger. He shot a mean glower toward the map room, his teeth clenched.

"It's time we got some answers."

Leash marched into the map room and strode straight up to Ramsey and May. He faced Ramsey point-blank.

"Something's got one of my men," Leash said. "I need to know what it is."

Ramsey slowly swiveled his head toward him. They locked a stare colder then the glaciers outside. May watched them with a tense face.

Leash could see tiny muscles rippling under Ramsey's face, but the man's withstood his stare. He was a tougher nut than Leash had thought.

"Captain, you have your orders—"

"No one here will move a finger unless you tell us what we're up against."

Leash's words hit like mortar shells. Ramsey's eyes narrowed to slits.

"This is mutiny, Captain."

The Rangers entered the room. One by one, they closed the ranks behind Leash like a human wall, staring at Ramsey with full-out menace. The air grew so thick with tension that even the wind outside backed off to a safe distance.

Ramsey reached for the pistol in his holster. In an instant, Hitch flipped up his knife and gripped it by the blade, ready for a throw.

"I wouldn't pull out that gun, sir."

Swollen veins pulsated on Ramsey's temples. His hand rested on his pistol's handle, wavering . . .

At that moment, May stepped in between Leash and Ramsey. She pushed Ramsey's pistol back into the holster.

"I'll tell them," she said. "We've got no choice."

Ramsey and Leash stood silent, eyes locked. Ramsey blinked. This time it was him who was weighing his chances. He stepped aside, jaws clenched.

"Next time I'll call your bluff, Captain."

With a calming gesture, May motioned Leash and the Rangers to sit down. They hesitated but complied.

May stepped before them. She removed a file folder from her dispatch bag, stamped *Top Secret*. From inside, she pulled out a copy of a medieval woodcut. She held it up for the Rangers to see. The woodcut showed an old man in wizard-like robes. The man sat in a wooden chamber filled with manuscripts and flasks. A string of occult sigils adorned the woodcut.

May spoke in a quiet, matter-of-fact tone.

"Five hundred years ago, a rabbi in Prague studied ancient scripts in a secret library called the Golden Chamber. Legends say he discovered how to bring to life a Golem."

"A what?" Hitch said.

"A living being made from non-living matter. A vengeful warrior who could fight for his people."

The Rangers traded perplexed glances. May presented another woodcut. This one showed a hulking figure made of clay. Two hollow eye sockets stared from a rough-hewn face.

"The rabbi put a secret word in the mouth of a clay figure. It came to life. The secret word was written in an ancient script called Old Malachim, the mythical language of angels."

She showed a few verses written in a stark, angular alphabet.

"What word was that?" Leash said.

"Anyone here read the Bible? John 1:1?"

"'In the beginning was the word,'" Rufus said, "'and the word became flesh.'"

"That's the one."

She pulled out another woodcut. It showed God as a bearded old man in the clouds. He was breathing life into Adam and Eve.

"The word God spoke to create the world."

The room fell silent, as if under the spell of a supernatural tale. The Rangers gaped at the woodcut with captive eyes.

"A year ago," May continued, "the Germans launched a secret project called *Durendal*. They found the Golden Chamber and brought it here to make a weapon."

"What weapon?" Leash said.

May glanced at Ramsey and paused, choosing words carefully.

"A fearless warrior who will fight for the Reich. A warrior who can't be killed because he's already dead."

The Rangers gaped at her, slack-jawed.

"No one has been able to crack the angelic script since the Middle Ages," May said. "Only recently, a professor of linguistics did it, after a lifetime of research." She looked away to hide the emotion flooding her face. "My father."

The Rangers gazed at her in silence. May took a deep breath.

"The Germans awakened the Golem to do evil, against the old commandments," she said. "But they forgot one thing: evil brings disobedience. The Golem turned against them." She sighed. "The hardest part about playing God is to not make a human mistake."

"Why did he wipe them out?" Hitch said.

"Any creation resents its creator. It wants his power."

"What is this Golem?" Leash said. "A ghost?"

Without a word, May showed another woodcut. A towering human effigy made of wooden logs was destroying a village, watched on by a horrified crowd. The effigy was alive.

"A manifestation. A force that can breathe life into matter."

Leash drilled May with an intense stare. Time for the question of the day.

"Can we destroy it?"

May shook her head, grim-faced. A murmur of unease rolled through the room. The Rangers gaped at May, astonished.

"Can we stop him?" Leash said.

May traded a furtive glance with Ramsey.

"According to legends, there is a way."

"What is it?"

"The rabbi took the secret to his grave. But he left a strange clue: a Latin psalm torn in half."

She showed another woodcut. In it, the rabbi stretched out his hands, holding two halves of a torn page.

"My father discovered one half hidden inside the cover of an old manuscript. The Germans must have found it when they kidnapped him."

From her dispatch bag, May pulled out a page from a notebook. Copied in pencil was a torn fragment of a short psalm.

"A few weeks ago I found the other half and made this copy. I studied it for days on end. Nothing, just an old, Latin psalm. Maybe you need both halves to crack the clue."

Leash rubbed his forehead, digesting the information. Questions stampeded through his mind. Too bad none of them made much sense. He struggled to find the right words. Hell, he'd ask in the simplest way.

"Does the Golem know why we came here?"

"He can sense it," May said.

"That means he'll try to stop us."

May nodded. A morose look crept onto her face.

"That's not the worst thing."

"I'm all ears," Leash said.

"His powers grow with each kill. If we don't stop him soon, there won't be any stopping him at all."

"What is it that he wants?" Leash said.

"Freedom from his maker."

May ran her gaze across the Rangers' faces.

"To get it, he'll shape himself in his image and learn his evil ways."

Hitch raised his eyebrows.

"His maker?"

"Man."

The word cut through the air like a bullwhip and echoed back for a while. The room sank into a gloomy silence.

CHAPTER V

"ALL RIGHT, men, let's wrap up here!"

Eiffel eyed the console with satisfaction. A tangle of welded wires crisscrossed the electric circuits inside. One of the techs slid the cover panel back in place. The others waited nearby, ready to go.

Eiffel turned on his Handie.

"We're done in the plant, sir. We're heading back."

Leash's voice rang with gloom.

"Listen to me carefully, Eiffel. Keep your head low and stick to the shadows. If you see any motion, do not engage! Head right back here! I repeat: do not engage!"

Eiffel's men heard it. They exchanged concerned glances. Fear glimmered in Eiffel's eyes.

"Is there something we should know, sir?"

"Can't explain this over the radio. Just do what I say, Eiffel."

"Copy that, sir."

Eiffel switched off his radio. His men eyed him with concern.

"You've heard the man. Let's move," Eiffel said.

The Rangers flung their guns over their shoulders and marched out of the power plant, unease on their faces.

The lights of the HQ building gleamed far in the distance.

The map room reeked of tension. The Rangers stood guard by the windows, eyes wide with anxiety, hands clawing their guns. They peered out into the dark surroundings. They knew something was out there. Unseen. Hiding. Dangerous. Would they even see it coming?

Leash, Ramsey, May, and Hitch leaned over a map of the base. Ramsey pointed to a spot.

"We suspect they are keeping the professor in the bunkers—"

Leash raised his hand, listening attentively.

"Quiet!"

Somewhere nearby they heard the ring of a phone. Leash frowned, surprised. A phone call? Here? He looked around, unsure if his ears were playing a trick on him.

The phone rang again. There was no doubt about it: someone was calling the headquarters.

"What the hell?" Hitch scratched his head.

They listened, ears perked to pinpoint the source. The phone rang again.

"The switchboard!" Leash leapt to his feet.

They rushed out into the hallway, rounded a corner, and burst into a small phone room. A phone switchboard hulked against the wall, big as a fridge. The upright Bakelite panel was divided into a grid of sockets, each neatly labeled in German black letter. One of the lights was flashing red. Leash looked closer. The socket was labeled *Der Bunker.*

"What do we do?" Hitch said.

Leash gripped a patch cord. He hesitated for a moment, nervously rubbing the cord. He then plugged it into the *Der Bunker* socket. A bullhorn-sized speaker mounted atop the switchboard crackled with static noise.

A brief silence. Then a man spoke up in English with a coarse, Bavarian accent.

"Good morning, *Herr Kommandant.* Or is it good evening? Hard to tell around these parts."

The Rangers traded looks of bewilderment. Leash leaned toward the microphone.

"Who are you?"

"Allow me to introduce myself," the man said, "*Hauptsturmführer* Carl Albers of the SS. Welcome to my headquarters. I say *my* because you can still see me right behind you."

Leash quickly spun around, as if expecting to see Albers in person. On the wall behind him hung a framed portrait of a German officer in his forties in a spotless black uniform and slicked-back brown hair. An Iron Cross with Oak Leaves dangled under his chin. His had the haughty stare of a man who had worked his way up the ladder over the bodies of others.

"How did you know we're here?" Leash said.

Albers burst into a belly laugh.

"It's not hard to see the only building with lights on, *Herr Kommandant.*" His laugh turned into condescension. "If I were you, I'd kill the lights. They lure moths, you know."

Leash bit his lips. Just what he needed, some stuck-up SS bonehead japing him. He covered the mike with one hand.

"Kill all lights outside!"

The lights in the HQ windows went out.

"We knew you weren't Germans," Albers said, "since you made no contact. May I know *whom* I'm speaking to?"

He put a stress on "whom." He must have been dying to show off his proper English picked up at some Bavarian SS academy. Leash suppressed a shudder. The prospect of exchanging pleasantries with some SS creep felt positively bizarre.

"Captain Leash, U.S. Rangers. Why are you calling?"

"By now you know what happened here. When the ghost broke loose, I locked myself in the bunkers with a few of my men. *And the professor.*"

He paused for effect.

"I propose an exchange. We give you the professor, you give us your half of the psalm."

Silence. Leash and May traded concerned glances.

"How do we know he's still alive?" May said.

"Oh, *Fräulein* Benedict? Nice to hear your voice."

May clenched her jaws. Leash wasn't surprised. The charm Albers put on was rather revolting.

"I anticipated your question," Albers said.

He barked something in German. They heard muffled moaning, like someone's gag being removed. Then a feeble voice.

"May, is that you?"

May jolted.

"Dad!"

"May, listen to me, they are—"

Albers cut him right off. "That's enough."

They heard the muffled moaning again.

"So what's it going to be, *Herr Kapitän?*" Albers said.

The phone room fell silent. May's eyes burned with distress. Leash scratched his chin. Finally, his faced lit up with decision.

"Where and when?" he said.

May opened her mouth. Leash gestured her to keep quiet.

"In the bunker mess hall, in two hours," Albers said. "If you try any tricks, the man dies. Understood?"

"Yes."

"I'll see you then, Captain Leash."

Albers hung up. May glared at Leash.

"What do you think you're doing?! You can't just give them—"

Leash raised his hand in a calming gesture. He had the tranquil look of a man who knows exactly what he's doing.

"We're not giving anything."

"What's your plan, Captain?" Ramsey said.

Ignoring Ramsey, Leash turned to May.

"Can you make a copy of the psalm and garble it enough to throw off the Germans?"

May stared at him, surprised. She nodded.

"Please get to work right away."

May stepped out of the room. Ramsey stood still for a moment, then followed in her footsteps.

Leash frowned and rubbed his forehead. *Wait a second.* Something wasn't right here.

Hitch took notice.

"Something's bothering you, sir?"

"I wonder how Albers knew we came here with the other half of the psalm."

"He said he'd seen the lights."

Leash shook his head and locked gaze with Hitch.

"I'm not asking how he knew we were here. I'm asking how come he knew we *had* the psalm?"

Hitch eyed him quizzically.

❈ ❈ ❈

Eiffel's squad marched into the yard before the HQ building. Eiffel glanced up and signaled his men to stop. The building before them loomed dark and silent, like a haunted mansion. All doors and windows were locked. All lights were out. Kaminski whistled.

"They shut the place tight like momma's pantry. Maybe the Krauts showed up?"

They peered around and firmed their grip on their guns. There was no one in sight. Eiffel turned on his radio.

"Dakota, this is Blue Seal, come in."

One of the windows on the upper floor squeaked open. The barrel of a gun peeked out, followed by the eyes of a hiding Ranger. The radio crackled.

"I-I-I-dentify yourself!"

"Your momma with hot cocoa. Open up, Mopey, it's Eiffel."

Mopey didn't move an inch. Instead, he watched them warily, his voice full of suspicion.

"What's your sign, Sarge?"

Eiffel's jaw nearly fell off. His men traded bewildered looks.

"What did you say, Mopey?"

"What's your sign, Sarge?"

"Mopey, what's your goddamn problem?! You know how cold it is out here?!"

"I'm so-so-sorry, Sarge. I need to-to know that you-you-you are really you."

Eiffel clenched his teeth.

"Virgo."

Mopey vanished from the window. The entrance door creaked open. Mopey stood inside, waving his arms around.

"Co-come in quick!"

He peered around fearfully, his gun aimed at the surroundings. Eiffel's men stepped in.

"What's with this damn cloak-and-dagger?!" Eiffel demanded.

"We've ha-had a shoo-shoo-shoot-out, Sarge!"

"Krauts?"

Mopey's eyes glinted with fear.

"So-so-something else."

Leash and Hitch entered Krause's room. Krause sat on his bunk, sipping hot soup. Slocombe stood nearby, his eyes aglow with intoxication. Leash eyed Slocombe.

"How is he?"

"He can talk sense, if that's what you mean, sir."

Leash sat down in front of Krause and fixed him with a leaden stare. Krause glanced up, then cast his eyes down again. He whispered under his nose.

"Thank you."

"For what?"

"You know . . . In the hallway."

"You can thank me by answering a few questions."

Krause kept his eyes on the soup can.

"I won't help you. I'm not a traitor."

"We can beat this demon only if we work together."

"I swore an oath to Germany—"

"Spare me the hooey," Leash's voice cut like a chain saw. "You swore an oath to a monster not much better than the one we're dealing with."

Krause's lips quivered.

"I . . . can't betray my nation."

Leash leaned over, his face only inches away from Krause's. He gripped Krause by his chin and forced him to lock gaze.

"Soldier, if this demon gets off this island, there *will be no nations.*"

Leash saw it in Krause's eyes right off. *Score.* The man was crumbling like haystack. Krause took a deep breath, his voice a resigned whisper.

"What do you want from me?"

Leash and Hitch traded a glance of triumph.

"Have you been to the weapons labs? Have you seen the captive professor?"

"The SS guarded the labs at all times. They never let *Wehrmacht* in."

"How many men does Albers have with him in the bunkers?"

"Only a few survived. Maybe six or seven."

Leash forced Krause to lock gaze again.

"You sure about these numbers?"

"Yes."

Leash got up about to leave. Krause grasped his hand, fear gathering in his eyes.

"Captain, please leave this place!"

Leash freed himself from Krause's grip.

"I can't." He pointed to the Ranger's insignia on his arm. "This badge came with a job description."

He signaled Hitch. They stepped outside.

"You believe him, sir?" Hitch lowered his voice.

"I've got no choice."

"What if it's a trap?"

"We've got to take a chance. Get everyone into the map room."

Hitch nodded and headed off. Slocombe sneaked out of his room and tiptoed toward Leash. He looked around to make sure no one was looking, then leaned over in a confidential whisper.

"Captain, why don't we just play along?"

"Play along?"

"You know, with the Germans," Slocombe continued. "Let's just give them what they want and get the hell out of here. There's no need to play heroes. No one will ever know. I can't stand this—"

He stopped mid-sentence. Leash pinned him down with a cold glower.

"I sure hope it's the morphine talking, Doc."

Slocombe put on a sheepish grin.

"Yes . . . of course."

Leash whirled and headed off. Slocombe bit his lips and shuffled back into his room.

May hunched at a desk in a windowless office. The room was small, painted a depressing Prussian blue; torn paperwork littered the floor. A framed photo of a German officer with a pudgy Hessian belle hung on the wall. Face tense in concentration, May was putting the final touch on a duplicate of the psalm.

Leash stood behind her, holding a blanket. She didn't hear him come in. He watched the frizzy brown hair on the crown on her head. The backlighting from the desk lamp made the hair look like a halo. Would an ice queen have a halo?

Without a word he wrapped the blanket around May's shoulders. She jerked, surprised.

"What's this?" she said.

"An icebreaker. Forgive the pun."

She smiled. Leash noticed the framed photo of her father beside her.

"Sorry about your father. I didn't know—"

Better not to finish the sentence. May stopped working and stared at the photo. Her face soured a bit. Her tone was tender and bitter at the same time.

"He always wanted a son. I was the only child, so he treated me like a boy. A substitute. He poured all his knowledge into me, so that one day I could succeed him . . ."

Leash kept quiet. He knew better than to interrupt someone on a confession binge. She sounded like she'd been dying to unload this for years. Preferably onto a complete stranger.

"In a way I'm my father's Golem." She sighed. "Now I get a chance to take on his only mistress: science. My rival from birth. Perhaps that's what drove me through those damn eight years of college."

The room plunged into silence. Leash stood motionless. How do you handle an outpouring like this? Best pretend it hadn't happen at all.

"So how's the psalm going?"

She shot him a grateful glance. He knew why. He didn't let her guard drop past the point of embarrassment.

She handed him the copy of the psalm.

"Should fool a layman."

"Can I see the original?"

May handed him the original. Leash put the copy on top of the original and held out the two against the light so as to see the changes. May looked ticked off.

"You don't trust me?"

Leash spied the changes made in the psalm. There were many. He folded one of the papers.

"I do. What I don't trust is details. And that's where the devil is."

He handed the folded paper to May and pocketed the other one.

"I'll keep the original. You keep the copy."

May frowned in protest.

"But—"

Leash raised his hand to calm her.

"I know what I'm doing."

He put on his best laid-back face to make it look like he was actually telling the truth.

"Please get ready to march out, Miss Benedict," he said and started toward the door.

"May," she said.

He stopped and glanced back at her. *No.* Positively not an ice queen.

"May."

He headed out.

The Rangers lined up in a row in the map room, their gaze on Leash. He stood before them, a tough mask on his face. If he could only rid his eyes of that damn glimmer of concern that had somehow slipped through.

The men picked up on it right away. It was one of *those* moments. Leash was about to play poker with fate. Their lives lay in the pot.

"Okay, men, here's the plan. We're splitting up. Mr. Ramsey, Miss Benedict, Hitch, Mopey, Jerome, and Rufus are coming with me. We're taking the German as a guide. The rest stay put. Eiffel takes command. Radio contact every fifteen minutes."

His voice dropped a notch.

"If we don't report for an hour: evacuate. A rescue plane will land across the mountains in twenty-four hours."

Better end the speech right there. Leash knew this might be the last time he saw some of his men, but there was no way to bid farewell and not turn it into teary-eyed mush. He knew his men didn't expect it, either. Silence is the only farewell that never sounds phony.

He turned to Hitch.

"Let's go."

Leash and his group filed out the front door. Before them lurked the ghost town of the base, tucked beneath the dark, polar sky. They marched off due east, boots crunching through the snow.

The remaining Rangers thronged by the door to see them off. No one uttered a word.

Finally, Eiffel broke the silence.

"Godspeed."

Leash couldn't hear him. He and his troop were already gone, the sound of their footsteps drowned by the howl of distant winds.

CHAPTER VI

LEASH AND HIS TROOP edged down a snow-swept road in combat formation. The dark silhouettes of the buildings lurked like a gauntlet of evil spirits. A cold wind whistled through the glass teeth of broken windows. Some unseen shutters swayed to and fro with a sinister squeak.

Rufus clutched the pocket Bible to his chest, muttering under his nose.

"And God made a man of clay and breathed into him a living soul . . ."

Hitch glowered at him. Rufus paid no attention.

"And then the man of clay made his own man of clay," he muttered on. "But that man was bereft of a soul, for man is not God and cannot grant soul to his creation—"

"Shut the hell up, Rufus." Hitch said.

"Because whatever man creates, he soon turns into a monster—"

"I said lay it off now! This jabber is getting on my nerves!"

Rufus gave him a cold stare.

"You're just jealous, Hitch."

"Come again?" Hitch's eyes glinted with menace.

"'Cause I've got a real reason to fight," Rufus raised his Bible. "And all *you* want is the damn pardon."

"You son—"

Hitch leapt toward Rufus. Leash jumped in and pulled them apart.

"Cool it, Hitch. We're all on edge."

Hitch stepped aside and took a deep breath through clenched teeth. Leash turned to Rufus.

"Do you believe in God, soldier?"

"Yes, sir," Rufus said, surprise in his eyes.

"You believe in the devil?"

"Yes, sir."

"Then buckle up, soldier, 'cause he's out there waiting for you." Leash pointed toward the base. "Are you ready for him?"

Rufus gaped at Leash, surprised.

"Are you?" Leash raised his voice a notch.

Rufus nodded.

Hitch stood a few steps away, his face still tense. He noticed May watching him.

"I don't need the pardon for myself, Miss," he said, a poignant look in his eyes. "It's for my little girl. Haven't seen her in five years." From under his parka's hood he pulled out the photo of his daughter and showed it to May. "See? I keep it close, so she's always on my mind."

Leash raised his hand.

"All right, let's—"

He stopped mid-sentence. Playing somewhere nearby was a sweet lullaby. They traded surprised glances.

"What the hell?" Jerome said.

The tune seemed to come down from heaven, as if a stray angel had decided to swing by to serenade them. Leash looked up. A loudspeaker hung atop a nearby pole. The gentle tinkling of a music box was playing through the base's PA system.

Hitch's eyes flashed in recognition.

"It's Gilchrist! He's calling for help!"

Leash grabbed Krause by the elbow. "Where is the PA room?!"

His hand trembling, Krause pointed to a cluster of barracks to the south. "In the crew barracks!"

Ramsey accosted Leash.

"Captain, we've got a job to do in the bunkers!"

Leash checked his watch.

"We've got twenty minutes to spare."

"But my father—" May's plaintive voice trailed off.

Leash's tone softened as he met her gaze. "I've got a wounded man out there," he pointed to the barracks. "I've seen his blood."

"What if it's a trap?" Ramsey pressed on.

"What if it isn't?"

Leash signaled the others. "Come on!"

The Rangers sprinted off toward the barracks. Ramsey and May followed, dejected.

❆ ❆ ❆

Slocombe peeked out into the hallway outside his room. It was empty. He slipped out, clutching a black leather bag. He sneaked down the hallway toward the stairway. He looked around once again, rushed downstairs into the basement, and stepped into a dingy utility room. The place was covered with piping and wiring. A lone bulb hung overhead. He sat on the floor and reached inside the bag. A morphine vial glinted in his hand. Slocombe eyed it with a greedy stare.

Eiffel scanned the map room. All lights were out, save for a few flashlights. His men kept watch by the windows, their weapons aimed at the surroundings. Vandover, a double-chinned corporal with a broken nose, crouched by a window, gazing up toward the sky. Kaminski sat on the floor nearby, greasing the lock of his Tommy gun. He chewed a wad of tobacco, his jaws bobbing rhythmically. Eiffel looked at their faces: tense, anxious eyes, waiting for something to happen. What? No one knew. Whatever it was, it would come from out there . . .

Eiffel's eyes drifted back to the deck of Tarot cards spread face-down before him. He picked up a card, turned it over, and shone his flashlight on it. His gaze froze.

Kaminski noticed.

"What is it, Sarge?"

Eiffel gaped at the card in his hand. *Death.*

"Nothing."

He switched off his flashlight to hide his worried face from others. He could do without their derisive glances.

Clank! Kaminski slammed the gun's lock shut to check the action. Vandover jerked, startled.

"Antsy, ain't ya?" Kaminski said.

Vandover kept staring out the window.

"Look at the stars," he said.

Kaminski followed his gaze. The sky was clear, like a tropical lagoon; a billion specks of light were splattered in bluish spirals, like a giant, painted circus tent. Kaminski whistled.

"Unreal, man. How come I never see this back home?"

"'Cause God ain't gonna waste this beauty on Jersey."

Kaminski let the jab slide. "Reminds me of a story I heard as kid," he said. "Two guys were crossing the Rockies. They had a few days left on the trail. As they camped out one night, they saw a light flickering far on the horizon. One of them says: hey, let's see what that is. The other one goes: no, we gotta stick to the trail. So they did."

Kaminski looked around. The story had grabbed the attention of the others.

"Next night," he continued, "they camp out again, and the light is still there, on the horizon. The first one says again: let's see what that is. The second guy goes: no, it's a waste of time. So they go to sleep. Next morning the second guy wakes up and sees that his friend's gone, gear and all. He yells after him and looks around. Nothing. He moves on. Next night he camps out, he looks toward the horizon and guess what?"

"There's a second light on the horizon, next to the first one," Vandover said without batting an eyelash.

Kaminski eyed him surprised.

"How d'ya know? You heard the story?"

"No. I was the guy in the Rockies."

The Rangers were just bursting into chuckles when—

"Watch out! He's coming!" Vandover yelled.

He let loose a fierce salvo into the darkness outside. Gunfire strobed across the room as the others blasted away in panic. Johanna thrashed her wings, scared by the noise.

Eiffel leapt toward the window. "Where?!"

"Storage shed, far left!"

Eiffel peered out through his binoculars.

"Hold your fire!" he yelled.

The barrage drowned his voice.

"I said *hold your fire!*"

The Rangers ceased firing. Eiffel cocked his flare gun and fired out the window. The flare whooshed through the air with a blinding red trail and plowed into the snow near the storage shed. The surroundings lit up with a ghoulish, red glow. A polar fox lay there in the snow, its bullet-riddled carcass still twitching in agony. Eiffel sent Vandover a peeved glower.

"Dead animal. Bad omen."

His Handie crackled.

"Sarge, I need you in the radio room," Julius said. "You've got to see this right away."

"I'm coming."

Eiffel stepped out, the look of anger still on his face. As soon as he was gone, Vandover put on a scowl, mocking Eiffel, and moved his lips in a silent parody: "Dead animal. Bad omen."

Eiffel stepped into the radio room. The casing was pulled off the radio. Julius hunched over, screwdriver in hand, squinting like a PI on a hot trail.

"What is it, Julius?" Eiffel said.

Julius pointed to the vacuum tubes.

"The wiring's cut up, sir. I'd checked the gear before we boarded."

Eiffel leaned over. The wires were broken in a few places.

"Could've burned through."

Julius pulled out the loose end of a wire and showed it to Eiffel.

"Clean cut with pliers. Someone must have done it when I got lured out of the room."

Eiffel locked gaze with Julius.

"You're saying we've got a saboteur?"

Julius nodded.

❊ ❊ ❊

The room in the crew barracks was pitch black. Someone or something peered out through a broken window. There was no telling who or what that was; just a vague silhouette against the sky. Far in the distance, Leash and his troop were approaching.

Leash crouched behind an armored carrier and peeked out. Fifty yards before him stood the boxy shape of the crew barrack. He watched it through his binoculars. The front door stood wide open, as if in invitation. Behind it stretched an impenetrable void.

Leash eyed Krause.

"Where's the PA room?"

"Deep inside, on the right."

Leash firmed his grip on the binoculars. He scanned the windows on the right, trying to pierce the darkness behind them. No dice.

"Damn, I can't make anything out."

He turned to his men.

"All right, we're going in. Two sides, three-man cover! Hitch, lay down a candlestick!"

They dashed toward the barrack in a pincer formation and lined up on both sides of the entrance, ready to move in. Hitch crept toward the door. He struck a flare and tossed it in. The hallway inside lit up with a ghastly green glow. Hitch peeked in.

"Clear!"

They stormed into the building, guns at the ready. Two dark hallways branched left and right, flanked on both sides by the crew's quarters. The place looked like a city ransacked by looters. Clothes and mattresses littered the floor, buried under a layer of scattered papers. The light from the flare cast long, sinister shadows up the walls. No one was around.

"Which way?" Leash whispered to Krause.

Krause pointed right. Leash shone his flashlight that way. He then pointed left.

"Check the other side, Mopey."

Mopey sneaked into the hallway on the left and soon vanished from view.

Leash turned to May and Ramsey.

"You two stay back with Rufus. Hell knows who's in there."

Rufus nodded. He, May, and Ramsey stepped aside and hid in a corner.

Leash and the others moved into the hallway on the right. They crept along until they reached a junction with a corridor. Krause pointed to the right.

"This way."

They were about to move when Leash signaled them to stop.

"Quiet!"

He listened intently. Hitch eyed him, puzzled.

"I don't hear anything, sir."

"Exactly. The music's gone."

The Rangers perked their ears and listened. Indeed, the music had stopped playing. What followed wasn't just a plain silence. It was the kind of morbid silence that follows when someone's heart stops beating. Their faces tensed up. Leash signaled them to move on.

"Keep your eyes open."

They edged deeper down the corridor until Krause gestured them to stop. He pointed to a door thirty feet ahead.

"PA room," he whispered.

The door stood ajar, the room behind it hidden in darkness. The frosted glass in the door was cracked and smeared with blood. The sign on the door read *Tonanlage! Zutritt verboten!*

Leash switched off his flashlight. Others did the same. Hitch started toward the door but Leash held him back.

"Wait till we get used to the dark. Whoever's in there has a leg on us."

Hitch nodded. They stood still for a while. Then Leash gave a signal.

"Rufus, Jerome, put a flank on it!"

The two sneaked up and took position on either side of the door, backs to the wall.

"Fingers on the wire!" Leash whispered.

They trained their guns at the room. Leash signaled Hitch and pointed to the bottom of the door. Hitch dropped to the ground, crept over, and pushed the door fully open with the barrel of his gun. The door squeaked. The Rangers stiffened, ready to fire . . .

Nothing happened.

Behind the door was a pigeonhole of a room, all in shadows. They could make out the bulky shape of a broadcasting console. A man sat motionless near it, his silhouette visible against the wall.

Leash eyed Hitch and flicked his fingers, mimicking the switching of lights. Hitch nodded. He thrust his gun up along the wall and hit the light switch. A light bulb came on. The Rangers blitzed into the room, guns trained on the seated man.

They froze.

The seated man was a Ranger, his head slumped on the console. His hand rested on a small music box, right next to the PA microphone. Hitch tiptoed over and gently tilted the Ranger's head back. His body gave off a horrid, squelchy sound. The man's throat was a bloody mess.

Hitch's eyes widened.

"Gilchrist?"

No response. Gilchrist lay still like a corpse. Hitch leaned over, apprehension in his eyes.

"Gilchrist, can you hear me? It's me, Hitch!"

Nothing.

"Gil—"

All of a sudden Gilchrist's eyes popped open, big and white like ping-pong balls. Hitch winced.

"Hhhhe . . ." Gilchrist struggled to speak. The air wheezed horribly through his mangled vocal cords. Hitch leaned closer.

"What?"

"Hh-h-he's here."

Gilchrist slumped dead on the console.

Mopey slunk down the dark hallway, his heart pounding like a piston. A faint streak of light seeped through an open door at the far end. He crept up and peeked in. Behind the door was a large locker room. Mopey slipped in, his finger on the trigger.

A lone light bulb hung in the center; a few broken tables and chair legs lay strewn about. To the right, brooms and shovels stuck out from a half-open closet. To the left, the room branched off into locker bank aisles. The aisles drowned in shadows.

Mopey stepped deeper into the room, his eyes scanning for the faintest sign of danger. He passed by the aisles, checking them over one by one.

Wham!

The door behind him slammed shut. Mopey dashed into a nearby aisle and hid in the shadows.

Unseen by him, a wispy tendril of vapor oozed in through the crack under the door and fanned out.

His body trembling in fear, Mopey watched the room through the open end of his aisle. For a few tense seconds, nothing happened. Then Mopey's eyes widened in awe.

The brooms, shovels, and broken chair legs on the floor began to *move by themselves*, commanded by an unseen force. They dragged across the floor with an ominous screech, pulling together toward a single spot off to the side. Mopey rubbernecked to follow the movement. No dice. That spot was beyond the locker bank, out of his eyeshot. Mopey could hear the objects clanking, as if they were stacking atop each other. A long, sinister shadow grew across the floor. Something or someone was rising off the ground. Hackles rose on Mopey's neck. The shadow had a human shape.

Mopey held his breath. He heard footsteps. Awkward, mechanical, lumbering. The figure casting the shadow stepped in front of Mopey's aisle, partly obscured by the locker bank. It was an eight-foot tall effigy made of wooden debris. It looked disturbing, like an ancient pagan idol or the armature for an unfinished sculpture of a man. It leaned on long, skeletal limbs, its openwork torso backlit by the hanging bulb. Its head was a just a misshapen lump of debris, yet its quick, alert movements were just as purposeful as that of a human. The figure was sentient.

What stood there was the Golem.

The wooden head swiveled toward the locker banks. Mopey shrank back into the shadows.

His lips let out an unconscious whisper.

"Jesus Christ . . ."

Mopey realized just how frightened he was: his stammering had vanished. A cold chill raked down his spine.

The Golem had no face. No expression. No eyes. The head was just a vague, dark contour. Yet Mopey could swear the ghost was staring right back at him, right into his eyes. He didn't understand how that was possible. He just knew it.

He backed deeper into the aisle, unable to take his eyes off this monstrosity. His hands nervously felt their way in the shadows. *There.* He found it. The door of the last locker was open. He slipped in and slowly closed its door, desperate to not make any noise. The door closed in silence. Mopey sighed. He'd made it. Thoughts blazed through his mind. Maybe he had a chance. Maybe the ghost hadn't seen him. Maybe the whole nightmare would just go away. He wiped the cold sweat off his forehead.

Than the worst happened . . . His radio crackled out loud.

"Mopey? You there?" Leash said.

God, why now?! Mopey killed the radio.

Too late.

The Golem spun his head toward the noise. He closed in on the entrance of Mopey's aisle and halted there, his backlit silhouette blocking any way out.

Holding his breath, Mopey peered through a row of air holes in the locker door. He wouldn't dare to move.

The Golem scanned the floor, as if looking for something. Nearby lay a shovel. The Golem turned his head toward it. The shovel lifted off the ground, sailed through the air, and fused with the Golem's arm to form a protruding weapon. The Golem stepped into the aisle and halted by the first locker.

Wham!

Without the slightest warning the Golem rammed the shovel through the locker, ripping a jagged hole in the door. He pulled out the shovel. The blade screeched horridly against the metal door. The Golem took a step forward.

Wham!

The shovel sliced through the next locker.

Fear drained all blood from Mopey's face.

The Golem pushed deeper into the aisle, skewering the lockers one by one, closing in on Mopey. The screech of pierced metal grew louder and louder, in a hellish, mechanical rhythm.

Mopey clawed the silver crucifix on his neck, fingers trembling in a palsy of dread, his panicked eyes on the approaching ghost. His lips quivered in a desperate prayer. He had no idea what he was saying.

" . . .hallowed be thy name, thy will be done on earth . . ."

Wham!

The Golem's shovel hit very close. *Too damn close.*
Mopey's face pulled taut, eyes aglare with determination. He knew he was a goner. But he wasn't going out
with a whimper, squashed dead like a fish in a can. A
man who can't win is a man who's got nothing to lose.
All he had to lose was two seconds of dignity.

Mopey kicked the locker door open and lunged out,
crucifix held high like a battle flag, his eyes closed tight.
He screamed at the top of his lungs with the kind of
overkill that only a mortal fear can call up.

"The Blood of our Lord protect me—"

He stopped mid-sentence.

Nothing happened. He waited a moment. Still nothing.
Then it dawned on him. He was still alive. He opened
his eyes. Slowly. . . He was alone. Only the gutted lockers nearby gave witness to what had just happened. His
locker was the only one left intact.

Mopey's eyes sparked with hope. God had given him
a chance to live. Why? He didn't know. There was no time
to waste. He bolted toward the door and pulled hard on
it. It was locked. Mopey looked around. He picked up a
crowbar, wedged it into the door frame, and tugged on
it to pry the door open.

Behind his back, the wooden debris that made up the
Golem's body quietly descended from its hiding place
atop the lockers. The pieces drifted down toward the
floor and silently assembled themselves back into the
eight-foot tall effigy.

A grin of triumph beamed on Mopey's face. The door
yielded by an inch. He was so close. Then . . .

Wham!

A mighty blow slammed the door shut. Mopey's
grin vanished. Still facing the door, he glanced up. A
long wooden limb stretched above his head, pinning
the door to its frame.

Mortal fear in his eyes, Mopey swiveled his head to follow the limb to its owner. He saw him soon enough. Two feet behind him stood the Golem.

Something glinted off to the side, at chest level. Mopey glanced over. The shovel blade at the end of the Golem's arm was ready to strike. Mopey closed his eyes.

Crrrack!

The shovel ripped straight through the door. Bloodied wood chips rained on the floor outside the locker room. A scream of agony echoed down the hallways.

Leash signaled the Rangers in the PA room.

"Quiet!"

They listened. A distant scream echoed throughout the barrack.

"It's Mopey!" Hitch's eyes widened.

The Rangers bolted out and raced down the hallway, boots thundering on the floor. They turned a corner into the hallway leading to the locker room and stopped in their tracks, eyes wide in shock. Sticking out of the locker room door was a bloody shovel.

"Mopey!" Jerome's voice was pure despair.

He sprinted toward the locker room.

"Jerome, wait!" Leash yelled.

Jerome burst into the locker room. The shovel blade jiggled, as Jerome wrestled to pry it free. *Crack!* - the blade broke off. The Rangers hurried into the room. Sorrow in their eyes, they watched Jerome set Mopey's mangled body down on the floor. Jerome kneeled, holding his brother's head in a tender embrace. A bloodied shovel handle lay nearby.

Leash signaled the others.

"Search the room."

The Rangers dispersed into the locker aisles. They soon emerged empty-handed, a grimace of pent-up anger on their faces.

"Nothing," Hitch said. "Just gutted lockers."

Leash looked around. On the floor in the center lay a pile of wooden debris. He frowned, headed over, and picked up a piece. He examined it. A broken chair leg. Nothing more. The image of Krause curled up in panic flashed through his mind.

"What is it, sir?" Hitch approached.

"Hell if I know."

Leash tossed the piece away. He hauled off and kicked the whole pile of debris asunder. The floor beneath was empty. Leash let out a heavy sigh, as if breathing had become a burden. What exactly had he expected to see? A grinning devil hiding beneath?

He clenched his teeth. There was nothing else they could do for Mopey. He checked his watch.

"We gotta move." He voice softened. "Come on, Jerome. We'll come back to bury him."

Jerome remained on the floor, hugging his brother, deaf and oblivious. It looked like Leash's voice hadn't registered at all. His eyes glazed over, as if the shock had turned the outside world into a mirage.

Grim-faced, the Rangers filed out of the room. Hitch nudged Jerome's shoulder.

"Come on, man. We'll come back."

Jerome shoved his hand off, his gaze firm on his dead brother. Hitch turned to Leash and spread his arms helplessly.

"Give him a minute alone." Leash whispered. "He'll come to."

Leash picked up Mopey's Thompson and flung it over his shoulder. He shuffled out the room, following the others.

Jerome was alone now. The clicking of the Rangers' footsteps outside soon faded out into silence. As soon as his comrades were far enough away, Jerome's face suddenly sprang to life. His eyes burned with vengeance, like Chinese firecrackers spinning out of control. The muscles on his face rippled up. He removed his brother's crucifix, hung it on his own neck, and gently closed his brother's eyes.

"See you in heaven."

He straightened up, flung his ammo belts over his shoulders, and picked up his M1919, all ready for action. Jaws clenched, he cocked the machine gun with a loud clank and marched out of the room.

"Where are you hiding, you sick bastard?!" he yelled into the dark hallways.

His voice echoed throughout the barrack. The Rangers stopped and listened.

"Sir, it's Jerome!" Hitch said.

CHAPTER VII

RAGE IN HIS EYES, Jerome blasted away from his machine gun as he strutted down the hallway. He lashed out blind salvos into the surroundings: the floor, the walls, the ceiling, everything. The slugs ripped through the doors and windows in a cascade of debris. Shells sprayed out of his gun like a fountain. The man was a berserker.

"Come on out, you goddamn beast, so I can spit in your face!"

The Rangers listened to the echoes.

"Sir, he lost it!" Hitch yelled.

Leash frowned, trying to pinpoint the direction of Jerome's voice.

"He's headed for the exit! C'mon!"

The Rangers sprinted down the hallways, guided by the noise. Rufus, May, and Ramsey sprang out from behind a corner, their faces tense.

"What's going on, sir?!" Rufus said. "We've heard a machine gun!"

"Jerome went bonkers!" Hitch said. He perked up his ears. "Sir, I think he just went out!"

Leash furrowed his brow, listening. Hitch was right. The noise was now coming from outside the building. Things were getting worse by the second.

They launched toward the exit.

"Jerome, get back in right now!"

Jerome burst out of the barrack, firing blindly into the snow. He swept the surroundings with furious eyes.

"Stick your head out, you goddamn devil!"

He ceased firing. His eyes froze, fixed on a strange phenomenon. About a hundred feet before him rose a pile of dug out ice. The huge ice blocks quivered for a moment, then moved by themselves, as if pulled by an unseen puppeteer. They came together and assembled themselves into a hunching, twenty-foot tall figure. It had a strange, off-kilter shape, like a cross between a centaur and an abstract sculpture. Its massive limbs, made of longer ice blocks, rested on the ground in bent arches, like an animal on the prowl. As soon as the figure took its shape, a quick jolt of energy passed through it. The figure steeled its stance in an act of conscious will, its actions commanded by a ghost within. The Golem awakened. He slowly swiveled his head toward Jerome. The Golem had no eyes. No face. Yet it was perfectly clear that he was drilling Jerome with a deadly stare.

Jerome peered around. He spied a massive tank hunched by the roadside. He sprinted over and climbed onto the turret.

The Rangers leapt out of the barrack and looked around. Their eyes widened in fear. Jerome stood atop the tank, facing off with a sentient giant made of ice.

"Jerome, what are you doing?!" Leash yelled.

Jerome dived down the turret hatch and slammed it shut. Leash quickly reached for his radio.

"Jerome, do you hear me?!"

Inside the tank, Jerome's Handie crackled with Leash's voice. Jerome paid no heed, his face scrunched in blind fury. He looked around. Tucked in a compartment below the turret lay a dozen cannon shells.

Eyes wide open, the Rangers watched on as the tank's turret began to swivel with a sinister hum. The cannon swept a half circle and came to a stop, pointed at the Golem like a giant accusatory finger. The Golem followed the motion with perfect indifference. Leash gripped his radio so hard, he almost crushed it.

"Jerome, get out right now!"

Wham!

As if in reply, the tank's cannon lashed out. The ground quivered. The shell hit one of the Golem's legs, shattering the ice blocks into powdery clouds. The Golem lost his footing and slumped sideways. But then . . .

The Rangers watched slack-jawed as the unthinkable happened. As soon the blast died down, the ice shards *reformed* themselves back into a leg. The Golem was again on his feet, as if nothing had happened at all. He eyed the tank with a clinical stare, like a surgeon scrutinizing a tumor.

Leash narrowed his eyes, his face tense with foreboding. He saw it coming. He yelled so loud that gobs of spit covered his radio.

"Jerome, for God's sake, cease fire! He's learning from you!"

Inside the tank, Jerome was in a battle frenzy, deaf to warnings. Face drenched in sweat, he jammed one more shell down the cannon breech and yanked hard on the firing lever.

"Die, you damned beast!" he growled through clenched teeth.

The tank fired again. This time the shell hit another leg. All in vain. The shattered ice blocks quickly pulled themselves back together. The Golem stood unscathed.

The radio rasped with Leash's screams.

"Jerome, you've got no chance!"

Grinding his teeth, Jerome peered around the turret, looking for something . . . something bigger. Something like . . . There it was. A big, tungsten-tipped shell glinted at him from the corner. Jerome's face lit up with a vicious grin. *That* should do it. He picked it up, all fifty pounds of jam-packed brass, and shoved it down the breech.

The Golem looked around. Jutting from the snow near the crew's barrack was a broken-off, four-inch thick icicle. The Golem focused his gaze on it. The icicle whooshed through the air and fused with one of the his limbs to form a protruding spike. The Golem turned toward the tank.

Leash held his breath, his eyes open wide. He knew something dreadful was about to happen.

Inside the tank, Jerome gripped the firing lever . . .

The Golem's limb shot forth like a snake's tongue and rammed the icicle down the tank's barrel, plugging it tight. Leash's eyes bugged out. He screamed into the radio.

"Jerome, *watch out!*"

Too late. Jerome pulled the firing lever.

Wham!

A deafening blast tore the turret inside out in a fireball of armor shards. The live shells went off in a chain reaction. The series of blasts had a kick so strong, the tank heaved off the ground for a split second. Leash and the others dropped for cover to dodge the whizzing debris.

The fireball died down. They raised their heads and gazed at the tank, pain in their eyes. The turret had vanished to its last atom. The tank was a smoldering crater.

The Golem now swiveled his head toward them.

"God, he's seen us!" Hitch yelled.

Leash peered around in despair. Every second mattered. Off to the side he spied a building marked with a red cross. He gripped May's elbow.

"Come on!"

They leapt to their feet and bolted off toward the infirmary.

The ice blocks that made up the Golem's body creaked ominously. Controlled by one will, the monstrous limbs shifted to assume an agile, beast-like shape. The Golem darted after Leash in a steady gallop, the ground shaking under him with loud thumps.

Hitch burst into the infirmary, leading the rest inside. Leash entered last and promptly locked the door behind them. He squinted at it and pounded on it to test its strength. The door gave off a feeble clonk.

"The damn thing won't last a second!"

He wheeled about and scanned the infirmary. It was a dim, large hall. Rows of bare bulbs dangled from the ceiling. All were out. The floor was littered with broken cabinets, medical gear, and upturned cot beds. Far in the back glinted the steel door of a storage annex. Leash wasted no time.

"Get behind the steel door!"

They all scurried across the room, trampling over the beds, and dived into the annex. It was a long, dark corridor lined with disused cabinets and medical machinery. An exit sign hung at the far end. Below it was a doorway, all hidden in shadows. They dashed that way, shone their flashlights in, and . . . stopped in their tracks, eyes open in a nasty surprise.

The exit was *bricked up.*

"We're trapped! It's a dead end!" May yelled.

Wham!

The sound of a violent crash came from behind them. They whirled in panic.

It took just one whack of the Golem's limb to smash the infirmary door and send its debris flying. The Golem peeked in through the door frame, his backlit head blocking the light from outside. He then squeezed the ice blocks that made up his body through the door frame and slipped in on all fours like a giant panther made of ice. He spied the open annex and dashed that way, his footsteps thudding across the floor.

"C'mon!" Leash yelled.

He and the others rushed toward the annex entrance. They thronged against the steel door and were about to slam it shut when . . .

Whoosh!

The Golem's icicle spike jabbed through the door crack like a demon claw. They threw in all their might to close the door. Veins popped up on their temples; their faces twisted in effort. No cigar. The icy claw kept thrusting in. It wedged itself deeper and deeper, trying to pry the door open. Leash looked around, desperate. Off to the side, a fire ax hung on the wall in a glass cabinet.

"The ax!" he yelled to May.

May spun around and shattered the glass with her elbow. She pulled out the ax and tossed it over to Leash. Leash gripped it and hacked off the spiky limb like a tree branch. It fell off and gave way. In an instant they slammed the door shut and latched it tight from inside with a heavy crossbar. Just as they breathed with relief . . .

Boom! Boom! Boom!

A series of powerful blows dented the steel door inward. The Golem hammered on it as if it were a punching bag. The door held firm. The blows stopped. Leash and the others listened attentively . . .

Nothing. Just dead silence.

"He gave up," Hitch sighed and mopped the sweat off his forehead.

They all slumped against the wall, exhausted. It took them a long time to catch their breath. Hitch eyed May, bleak-faced.

"I sure hope you can crack the riddle, Miss," he said, "'cause there ain't no weapon I know that can take that demon down."

May returned a gloomy stare.

"You can never take him down. He's inside us."

"I don't follow, Miss." Hitch gaped at her, baffled.

"I didn't tell you why the rabbi concealed the secret. He didn't want the Golem revived ever again, because he found out what the Golem was made of." She paused and lowered her voice. "Human fear. Human hate. Human evil. The corrupt soul of mankind."

Hitch watched her, speechless. May pointed toward the door.

"What you're fighting out there . . . is *yourself*."

The room drowned in a grim silence. It took a while for her words to sink in. Hitch was the first to gather his thoughts.

"Miss, I don't follow. Are you saying he's not real?"

"He *is*."

"But how can it be? If this ghost, this, whatcha call it, *manifestation*, is made of fear and evil, how can it exist? I mean here, in the real world?"

May locked gaze with Hitch.

"Are you afraid of him?"

"So what if I am?" Hitch was taken aback.

"If a surgeon cut you open and looked for your fear, would he be able to find it?"

Hitch slowly shook his head.

May kept her somber gaze on him. "Does this mean your fear doesn't exist?"

Silence fell on the room again. Leash rubbed his forehead, digesting May's words.

"If what you say is true," he said, "then there *is* no way to get rid of him forever."

May nodded. "We can only shut him down."

"We're *not* shutting him down," Ramsey said.

All eyes turned toward him. Ramsey's voice was cold as the winds outside.

"Our orders are to investigate this phenomenon and try to bring it under our control. We'll shut it down only in the worst case scenario."

"*Worst case scenario?*" Hitch nearly choked. "Like what? The end of the world?"

Leash drilled his eyes into Ramsey.

"What do you mean, 'bring it under control?'"

"We want to have him fight on our side, Captain."

"This monster? On our side?"

The sheer nonsense of this idea hit Leash like a hailstone. He shook his head in disbelief and looked at Ramsey as if the man had come from another planet. "What exactly *is* our side, Mr. Ramsey?"

"Your country, Captain," Ramsey glowered back.

"I thought you meant the War Department."

The words came out even more sarcastic than Leash had planned. He and Ramsey stared off like stags about to clash. May's gaze flitted between them with unease. She climbed to her feet.

"Come on, we better search this place." Her tone was calming. "There's got to be a way out."

She headed off and began to scour the annex. The others hesitated, then joined her.

The Golem stood still in the infirmary, gazing at the door before him. He leaned over to examine the frame. Right next to it was a vent covered with a grill. The Golem stretched his arm toward the grill. A tendril of cold vapor came off the ice blocks that made up his hand and oozed through the grill into the vent.

Teeth clenched in anger, Rufus raked through a medical cabinet in the annex. Nothing but vials and bottles. He shoved them off the shelf. They shattered on the floor in a crystal starburst. The others looked at him. Rufus burned with ire.

"There *is* no way out of here! We're trapped for good!"

"Easy there, Rufus." Leash watched him with concern. Last thing they needed was another man breaking up.

Rufus slumped on the floor, took a deep breath and covered his face. "What the hell does he want?"

"He knows we came to shut him down," May said quietly. "If you'd been dead for ages and one day you woke up, would you give up your life?"

Leash eyed May, surprised. He wasn't sure what to make of May's tone. She sounded . . . *motherly.*

"People take twenty years to grow up," May said. "By the time we do, we take life for granted. We can't remember our birth." She paused. "He does."

Leash squinted at her.

"You sound like you feel sorry for him."

May looked away, averting his gaze. She opened her mouth, about to speak when . . .

"He's coming in!" Hitch yelled.

They spun toward the door. A tendril of vapor was creeping into the annex through a duct by the door. Hitch looked around with despair.

"Goddamn it! We'll need a bomb to get out!"

Leash furrowed his brow and shone his flashlight toward the bricked-up exit.

Wait a second . . . A *bomb?*

The word struck him like a revelation. He quickly scanned the medical equipment strewn about the annex. There it was. A pile of metal tanks, each labeled with a flame symbol and the words: *Sauerstoff! Feuergefähr!* Leash pointed them out to May.

"What does it say?!"

"Oxygen."

Leash's eyes sparked with a fighting spirit.

"We're gonna blow up the exit! Take cover!" he yelled.

The others gaped at him without comprehension. Leash had no time to waste. He pointed to a big, metal-topped exam table standing by the wall.

"Come on, damn it!"

His roar whipped them into action. They darted over to the exam table and tugged on it to tip it over. Leash gripped a gurney and aimed it at the exit. He picked up a few oxygen tanks and dropped them on the gurney.

The tendril of vapor kept streaming out of the duct. It drifted through the air toward the latch bar . . .

Whomp!

Toppled by Leash's companions, the exam table thudded onto the floor, its metal-clad top toward the exit. They promptly took cover behind it and eyed Leash with puzzled glances. Leash tried to push the gurney toward the bricked-up exit. No luck. A tangled mess of cables sprawled on the floor held the gurney back. Leash gritted his teeth.

"Damn it!"

He tugged furiously on the cables.

Behind his back, the tendril of vapor had already enveloped the latch bar. The bar jiggled and rattled against the retainer, trying to free itself. Hitch looked that way. His eyes widened in disbelief.

"He's opening the door from inside!" he yelled.

Leash and others followed his gaze. The latch bar was sliding off the retainer, about to come loose.

Leash tugged on the tangled cables like a maniac. "Come on, already!"

Finally, the cables gave way. Leash braced himself and pushed the gurney down the annex, sped up, and let it loose at full speed. The gurney highballed toward the exit, clattering like a runaway train. Leash dropped behind the exam table and trained his gun on the oxygen tanks, his finger tight on the trigger.

Clank!

On the opposite end of the annex, the latch bar slid off the retainer and hit the floor. The door stood unlocked.

Standing just outside the door, the Golem hauled off, ready to punch the door open.

The gurney crashed into the exit so hard that its rear bounced up. Leash loosed a slug into the tanks and ducked for cover.

Blam!

A violent blast tore the bricked-up wall asunder. A hail of cinder blocks clattered against the walls. The blast spawned a billowing, fiery shock wave. It blew straight back down the annex like a belch from hell, skimming over the metal table. The narrow corridor focused it like a cannon.

With a mighty blow, the Golem bashed the annex door in. The door swung open and . . .

The Golem stopped in his tracks. Coming straight at him was a wall of fire.

The shock wave burst out of the annex like a tornado. All windows shattered and peppered the floor with a crystal shower. The impact knocked the Golem off his feet. He reeled back and tumbled on the floor like a tenpin. The ice blocks that made up his limbs twisted around with a loud screech and slid apart like dislocated joints.

The blaze in the infirmary had died down. Broken glass and debris lay strewn about the floor. The Golem reformed his body, climbed to his feet, and rushed into the annex. Halfway through, he looked ahead and slowed down. The exit was now a gaping hole. Behind it stretched a yard. The Golem lumbered toward the hole and peeked out. The yard was empty and silent; only winds howled somewhere in the distance. Leash and the others were gone. The Golem stood still for a few moments, then backed into the annex like a snake retreating to its lair.

CHAPTER VIII

A ROW of storage sheds and transformer stations surrounded the yard behind the infirmary. Hunching behind
them was a squat, boxy radar station. A grove of radio
masts and antennas sprouted from its roof. Toothy icicles
hung off the masts at sloping angles like saw blades.

Inside, the station was one big control room. Wrecked
radar consoles lined the walls. A panoramic bay window
stretched all around, affording a good view of the base.
Leash and the others reclined on the floor, their backs
against the consoles. They panted heavily, as if they'd
just outrun the devil. Ramsey lay on the floor, grimacing
in pain and clutching his bloodied leg.

Leash turned to Ramsey and opened his mouth to
say something . . . He hesitated. He wasn't too keen
on showing concern for the man. Ramsey had rubbed
him the wrong way, twice over. But he was in his troop.
Leash could feel the captain's bars weighing down on
his shoulders.

"You're hit?" he said.

Ramsey nodded.

"Must have been . . . the blast." He strained to speak through the pain. "I can't walk. Go without me. I'd be a burden . . . in the tunnels."

For the first time, Leash agreed with Ramsey one hundred percent. Leash weighed the options. He couldn't leave Ramsey alone here, that's for sure. He'd be gone within an hour.

"Stay with him," Leash eyed Rufus. "We'll come back as soon as we can."

Rufus nodded; a grimace of displeasure passed through his face. Leash noticed. Apparently, he wasn't the only one allergic to Ramsey's company.

Leash switched on his Handie.

"Dakota to Blue Seal, Dakota to Blue Seal."

"Copy, sir," Eiffel said. "Everything okay?"

"Just had a brush with the goddamn devil. Barely made it out alive. Mopey and Jerome are down. Ramsey's wounded. You're holding up down there?"

Eiffel lowered his voice to a confidential whisper.

"Sir, I need to tell you something. Julius discovered—"

Just outside the HQ building, a wounded Ranger crawled through snow toward the entrance. He was on his stomach, face buried in snow, barely alive, his parka all torn and bloodied. He was breathing so hard his next gasp could be his last. With all the strength he could muster, the Ranger writhed his way to the entrance door. He raised his frail arm, about to knock.

Kaminski stood guard on the other side of the entrance.

Knock . . . Knock, knock . . .

The tapping on the door had a broken, desperate rhythm. His gun at the ready, Kaminski peeked out through a side window. A Ranger lay motionless on the ground, the snow around him dyed blood-red.

"Sarge, we've got a wounded troop outside!" Kaminski yelled toward the map room. He noticed the name patch on the wounded man's parka. "Sir, it's Jerome! He's hit bad!"

"Let him in!" Eiffel yelled back.

Eiffel was busy fighting Johanna. She thrashed her wings in a sudden fit of panic, eyes popping out in fear. Then she bolted off and perched on a rafter in a dark corner, as if hiding from danger.

"Damn it, what's wrong with you, girl?" Eiffel said.

Kaminski opened the door. The wounded Ranger lay at his feet, face unseen . . .

Leash's radio crackled with Eiffel's voice.

"Sir, Jerome just made it back here. We're bringing him in."

Leash furrowed his brow. He wasn't sure he'd heard Eiffel right.

"Jerome? . . ."

His eyes widened in horror. A flash insight hit him like a thunderbolt.

"Close the door, Eiffel!" Leash roared, his spittle showering the radio. "You hear me?! Close it right now!"

"But, sir, Jerome—"

"It's *not* Jerome!"

Kaminski leaned over to grip the wounded Ranger by his shoulders. His eyes bugged out. A huge figure made of ice blocks shot up from underneath the snow like a volcano. It rose up till it turned into a twenty-foot monstrosity braced on long, sinuous limbs. The empty uniform fell to the ground. It was just a camouflage.

Kaminski stood still, his jaws slackened, his eyes glued to the dreadful sight. The Golem stared back at him.

Leash hollered into his radio.

"Eiffel? Did you hear me?!"

There was no reply. The radio crackled with gunfire, screams and the terrified screech of Johanna. Leash darted off toward the bay window and peered through his binoculars toward the HQ building. Muzzle bursts strobed in the dark windows like flashes at a boxing match. The bursts got shorter and shorter. Johanna's screech ended abruptly, as if the bird had been silenced.

"Eiffel? You there?"

The gunfire in the HQ building died down. The lights went out. The radio fell silent. The silence rang in Leash's ears like a train horn.

Hitch leapt to his feet, hands clawing his Tommy gun, itching to bolt out.

"Sir, we gotta—"

Leash grasped him by the shoulder.

"They're gone, Hitch."

Hitch freed himself from Leash's grip and stepped aside, face grim like a death mask. He took a deep breath.

"Come on," Leash said quietly. "We've gotta reach the bunkers."

Hitch gritted his teeth, eyes burning with rage. He flung his gun over his shoulder and headed out. May and Krause followed. Ramsey remained on the floor, guarded by Rufus. Leash was about to head out—

"Take this, sir."

Leash turned around. Rufus held out his pocket Bible, an earnest look on his face. Had it not been for what just happened, Leash would have scolded him. But at that moment the gesture made some inexplicable sense. Leash pocketed the Bible and left with the others. Rufus's somber gaze drifted off toward the HQ building.

❊ ❊ ❊

Leash and his companions peeked out from behind a stack of empty crates. They were at the eastern end of the base. Fifty yards before them loomed the fortified entrance to an underground tunnel, flanked by two massive pylons. The tunnel led straight down into the bowels of earth, its end vanishing in a pitch-black void. Leash couldn't shake off the feeling he'd seen something just like this before. He couldn't quite place it . . . Then he remembered: a yellowed photo of an Egyptian temple he'd seen in a newspaper. All that was missing were the giant statues of pharaohs.

"'Abandon all hope ye who enter here,'" May whispered to herself, her eyes on the entrance.

"Come on," Leash gave a signal.

They dashed toward the entrance and zipped down a staircase into a maze of underground tunnels. The murky tunnels were carved right into permafrost, with enough clearance for a truck. The rough-hewn walls glistened in shades of blue, punctuated by long strings of light bulbs. Cables and piping webbed along the walls like the blood vessels of a frozen dinosaur. Off to the side, a few mine cars idled on the rails. Broken tools and equipment lay strewn about. Leash peered around.

"Which way?" he whispered to Krause.

Krause pointed down a branching tunnel. They headed over. Flashlights in hand, they crept alongside the icy walls. May bumped into a rigid object protruding from a niche in the wall. She aimed her flashlight that way and winced in disgust.

"God . . ."

A mauled German soldier lay frozen in a machine gun nest, his fingers still clawing the trigger. The barrel pointed down the tunnel like a bared sword. Hitch leaned over for a closer look.

"Must've been a hell of a surprise when the demon broke loose."

"Come on. Let's go," Leash said.

They moved deeper into the tunnels. The place was silent like a tomb, each of their steps echoing back with pristine clarity. Krause led them, glancing from time to time at his sketched map. When they reached a junction, Krause stopped. He pointed into a tunnel branching off to the left.

"The mess hall," he whispered.

Leash looked that way. At its end was a half-open door labeled *Speisesaal.* Behind the door was a black void. Leash signaled the others to keep quiet. They sneaked toward the door and peeked in.

The mess hall was soaked in darkness. All lights were out. A few faint highlights glinted off metal-topped dining tables arranged in rows. Vague contours of kitchen equipment lined the walls. Leash and his troop slipped in, flashlights in hand.

"Keep your heads down," Leash whispered, "Hell knows who's in here."

They crept deeper into the hall, hunched close to the ground, dodging tables and scattered dishes. Leash stopped, his brow furrowed in concentration.

"Listen!" he whispered.

A plaintive moan was coming from the opposite end of the hall.

"*Captain . . .*"

The male voice sounded American, tinged with a Southern drawl. Leash and the others traded puzzled looks. The man moaned again. His voice was feeble, as if he had a hard time speaking.

"It's . . . me . . ."

Hitch frowned, rubbing his forehead.

"I know that voice . . ." he whispered. "Rufus? Is that you?" he called out to the moaning man.

Leash shushed Hitch and gave a signal to move on. Weaving in between the tables, they inched deeper into the hall. From behind an upturned table Leash shone his flashlight around the floor toward the moaning man. The light picked out a body in the dark. A Ranger. He lay on the floor by the opposite wall, barely alive. A wide, red splotch marked a gunshot wound in his chest.

Leash's eyed widened in surprise.

"Rufus?"

Rufus slowly rolled his eyes toward Leash and mustered all his strength to speak.

"It's a . . . trap . . ."

It took a split second for Leash to react.

"Let's get out of here!"

Too late. All lights came on with the flick of a switch. Leash and his companions froze, faced with a grim sight.

On the other side of the mess hall, right next to the wounded Rufus, stood Albers with five SS men, their guns trained on Leash. Next to Albers stood . . . Ramsey, beaming with health, his leg not hurt in the least. May's eyes opened wide. Her voice dropped to a stunned whisper, as if she were questioning her senses.

"Ramsey? . . ."

Ramsey flashed a smug grin.

"Around here, they call me Agent One."

Leash shot Ramsey a scowl. How he wished he could pry that smirk off Ramsey's face. Judging by the man's tone, Ramsey was all cock-a-whoop about the act he'd pulled off.

Albers stood silent and alert. He was in no mood for gloating. He pierced May with an iron stare.

"Take the others' guns, Miss Benedict. *Very* slowly."

Helplessness in her eyes, May collected guns from Hitch and Krause. When she turned toward Leash, he met her gaze and flitted his eyes down in a conspiratorial cue. May looked down. She saw it right away. Leash had two Tommy guns. Mopey's, flung across his back, was the one Albers saw. Leash held his own gun in his hand, behind an upturned table. The Germans couldn't have seen it.

May nodded a quick "got it."

"Hurry up, *Fräulein* Benedict," Albers said.

Her fingers quivering, May collected only the gun off of Leash's back.

"Now drop them," Albers said. "Be careful."

May dropped the guns on the floor a few feet away. Leash shot her a quick glance of appreciation. The trick worked like a charm. If fate could only grant them a split-second chance . . . Leash knew it wouldn't be easy. Albers kept his watchful eyes on them.

"Now all of you get up, hands above your hands," he said.

Out of the view from the Germans, Leash laid his gun across his feet. Hitch looked askance, catching a glimpse of what Leash was doing. They all rose up from behind the upturned table, their hands held high. Unseen by the Germans, the wounded Rufus regained a bit of strength. He looked around feebly. Leash saw it, but kept a poker face to not alert the Germans.

Ramsey wiped a splotch of red liquid off his pants. He showed off his stained hand, the smug grin still on his face.

"Fake blood, Captain Leash. Never fails."

"Why did you do this?" May said.

Leash's eyes glinted with appreciation. *Good call.* May caught on to his plan and was stalling. Ramsey bit the bait.

"Good income, Miss Benedict. The Germans had everything but your half of the psalm. I organized this mission not to stop the Germans, but to give them the missing piece. Which you delivered in person."

His vainglory sickened Leash. Ramsey reminded him of a snotty Boy Scout bragging about his brand new tracker badge.

Hitch sent Leash a furtive glance. Leash glanced back and saw that Hitch still had his knife at his belt. Leash rolled his eyes up toward the lights. Hitch nodded.

Ramsey was done crowing. The smirk vanished from his face, replaced by a tough, no-nonsense stare. He stretched out his hand toward Leash.

"The psalm."

May traded quick looks with Leash and reached into her dispatch bag. Ramsey's voice stopped her cold.

"No. I want the original." He drilled his eyes into Leash. "Captain?"

May bit her lips in disappointment. Leash paused and slowly pulled the folded paper from his pocket.

"We don't have the whole day, Captain."

Leash tossed the paper across the room to Ramsey. Ramsey snatched it mid-air.

"Thank you."

"Is that all we need?" Albers eyed Ramsey.

Ramsey nodded. Albers signaled an SS man. The SS man stepped forth and cocked his gun with a menacing clank.

Leash made quick eye contact with Rufus. Unseen by the Germans, Rufus reached toward his holster. His .45 was still there. Rufus quietly pulled it out. Leash's eyes flitted toward the advancing SS man. Rufus nodded.

"Sorry, Captain." Ramsey's face beamed with self-content. "You can't always be on the winning side."

Rufus trained his pistol on the SS man.

Leash nodded a "go".

"Damn right," he said.

Bang! Rufus knocked the SS man off. A split second later, Hitch flung his knife across the room and straight into the light switch. The switch shorted in a spray of fireworks. All lights went out, the metal tabletops glinting in the dim criss-cross of the dropped flashlights. The Germans lashed out in a blind fire, their muzzle flashes strobing like a flickery silent movie. Confused, they nearly did themselves in.

"*Verdammt!* Watch your fire!" Albers yelled.

Leash wasted no time. He kicked up the gun on his feet and caught it mid-air.

Albers leveled his pistol at Rufus and shot him dead. Leash saw this in the strobing gunfire, his eyes wide in horror. There wasn't much time for mourning. The Germans were rebounding from the surprise.

Leash gripped the table before him.

"Knock it over!" he yelled to his companions.

They toppled the table over to form a barricade. The SS men blasted away. Their bullets hammered the metal-clad tabletop, sparks flying all over. Stray slugs tore through the dish stacks at the back wall in deafening cascades of smashed porcelain. Leash fired back from behind the table, nailing one of the SS men in the chest. The man whirled and keeled over. Leash was far from triumphant. He knew full well they weren't going to last long behind that table. He peered around, desperate. On the wall behind them was the hatch of a food disposal chute.

"Drop down the chute!" he yelled to May. "We'll give you cover!"

May nodded. Dodging bullets, she slalomed over to the hatch. She gripped the handle and pulled on it. No cigar. The hatch was jammed.

One of the SS men spied a broken cabinet with fire equipment. He ripped open the cabinet door and removed a fire ax. He veered off from the others and crept along a side wall toward Leash's barricade.

Leash glanced at May, worried. She tugged on the hatch so hard, her face flooded red like a ripe tomato. The hatch wouldn't budge an inch.

"Come on!" Leash hollered.

May's sweaty hand slid off the handle and snagged a metal edge. She screamed as blood gushed out of her cut wrist. "I'm doing what I can!"

Leash turned to Krause. "Give her a hand!"

Krause rushed over to the chute hatch. He pulled May aside, swung his combat boot, and gave the hatch a solid kick. The hatch dropped open with a loud clank. May flinched and grasped her nose, face twisted in disgust.

"God, what a stench!"

Leash had not time for this.

"Get in right now!"

May clambered into the hatch and slid down the chute with a loud scream. Krause clambered in behind her. He was halfway in when a bullet whizzed by, tearing through his chest. A jet of blood sprayed out of his lungs. Krause slumped down, his life fleeting out of him. Leash saw it.

"Hitch, give him a hand!"

Hitch darted over and braced Krause up, helping him get all the way in. Krause plummeted down the chute like a sack of potatoes. Hitch stepped into the chute himself.

Leash peered out from behind the tabletop. Bullets whizzed by like tsetse flies. *Holy damn.* He was drawing all the fire now. The SS men charged toward the barricade, laying down a merciless barrage. The one with the ax was sneaking up on Leash from the side. When he was only a few feet away, he dashed toward Leash and hauled off. Hitch saw him in the nick of time.

"Sir, watch out!"

Leash rolled over just as the man's ax struck so hard, it got wedged in tabletop. Leash trained his gun at the German, pulled the trigger and . . . The gun clanked empty. Leash froze. *Bad, bad, bad.* The German sneered. Leash, desperate, glanced at his gun. The damn thing could still serve as a club. He swung it like a baseball bat and socked a good one on the sneering mug. The German keeled over in pain, holding his bloodied teeth.

"Sir, they're coming!" Hitch yelled.

Leash swiveled his head. The Germans were closing in fast. He had two seconds left, maybe three.

"Get in!" Leash yelled to Hitch.

Hitch dropped down the chute. Leash bolted out from behind the table, zigzagged toward the chute, and dived headlong into the hatch.

The Germans sprayed the hatch with bullets and rushed over. When they were just a few yards away, Albers raised his hand.

"Wait!"

They stopped and listened attentively. They heard a clangor which grew louder and louder. It sounded as if a small, hard object was traveling up the chute, bouncing off the walls. All of a sudden a hand grenade sprang out of the hatch and fell on the floor, spinning like a Chinese firecracker. Albers's eyes bugged out.

"Get down!"

The Germans hugged the ground. The grenade went off in a cracking blast, shrouding the hall with a veil of smoke. When the blast died down, the SS men leapt to their feet, rushed toward the chute, and flapped their hands to drive away the smoke. Stunned, they gaped at the sight before them. The blast had turned the hatch into an impassable tangle of twisted metal. Albers kicked the hatch with fury. Ramsey held him back.

"We got what we wanted," he said. "Let's get out."

Ramsey and the Germans hurried out. Behind them, the smoke lingered in the air like London fog.

❀ ❀ ❀

The tunnel was dark and cold like a morgue. All that was missing was a row of body drawers. Leash, Hitch, and May recuperated in a dark niche, panting, their breaths oozing out in eddies of vapor. Their faces were filthy, their parkas covered in slime, their hands bruised. Krause lay sprawled on the floor, pale as plaster, his chest torn in a blood-soaked mess. Hitch eyed him with a hopeless gaze.

"He took a bad one, sir," he whispered to Leash. "I think the lungs already collapsed."

Krause opened his mouth, wheezing hard for air. He rolled his eyes toward Leash and spoke in a choppy whisper.

"Captain . . . I don't think . . . I'll make it . . . before I . . . I need to tell you . . ."

Leash leaned over to hear him better.

"There's a ski plane . . . in a hangar . . . across the bay . . . A pilot waits for Albers . . ."

Leash and Hitch exchanged surprised glances.

"I didn't say this before . . . because . . . I don't want to be a traitor."

Krause struggled to put on a faint smile. He almost got there. His face stiffened, his eyes glazed over. He ceased to breathe. For a few moments Leash, May, and Hitch watched him in a grim silence. Without saying a word, Leash pulled Rufus's Bible from his pocket, set it down on Krause's chest, and wrapped Krause's fingers around it. The feeble half-smile still beamed from Krause face.

"Let's go," Leash said quietly.

They climbed to their feet, getting ready to march out. May gazed off down the tunnel. Its end vanished in darkness. She sighed with dejection.

"What do we do now?" she said. "We've lost our half of the psalm."

Her face had the dreary look of someone who had lost all hope.

"We didn't," Leash said.

May and Hitch whirled toward him, surprised.

"Albers knew we'd come here with the psalm," Leash said in a calm, matter-of-fact tone. "There were only two people who knew this when we arrived." He turned to-ward May. "You and Ramsey. Had you been a German spy, you wouldn't have garbled the copy. You did. That left only one."

May reached into her dispatch bag and pulled out her copy of the psalm.

"I switched them," Leash said. "What Ramsey has is the garbled copy."

May gaped at the psalm, astonished. Leash took her by the elbow.

"Come on. We've got to find your father."

They started down the tunnel. Behind them, darkness fell on Krause's body. With the Bible in his hand and the misty smile on his lips, he looked like a statue of a saint hiding in a niche of a Gothic cathedral.

CHAPTER IX

THE COMMAND BUNKER was grim and stark, like a medieval dungeon with industrial décor. German maps of the North Atlantic plastered the walls. A bulb dangled from the ceiling, keeping the corners in the shadows. Two SS men stood guard at the door. Albers and Ramsey leaned over a desk, poring over the two halves of the psalm. Ramsey carefully placed both pieces next to each other, edge to edge. His eyes raced down the verses . . . reading . . . re-reading . . . searching for clues . . .

"It's got to be something in—"

His brow furrowed in deep suspicion. He pounded on the desk, his eyes flaring up with ire.

"Damn it! They gave us the fake!"

"How do you know?" Albers said.

"They words don't match across!"

He pointed to the first half of the psalm. It ended mid-sentence. The second half of the psalm started with an initial.

Albers squinted at him, riled.

"You said getting the other half would be easy."

"I swear he had the original! He must have—"

Albers cut him off with a sweep of a hand. "No point arguing now."

He scratched his chin, pondering. A spark of menace glinted in his eyes.

"Come on," he said through clenched teeth. "We'll get them on their way out."

They hurried out of the bunker.

The tunnel maze grew bigger with each turn, the passages branching left and right like a mole colony. Leash, Hitch, and May marched down a tunnel, slogging through debris.

"You know, I've been wondering," Leash turned to May, "You said your father was the only one who cracked the old script. Why did he reveal the word to the Germans?"

"They must have threatened him."

"You also said your father had spent all his life deciphering it."

"So?"

"You're saying when finally got a chance to bring the Golem to life, he nobly refused?"

May halted, her cold eyes on Leash.

"What are you trying to say?"

"That temptation is all around us. Just like that damn ghost."

May opened her mouth to retort, but Hitch cut her off.

"Damn it, we're going in circles! I saw this sign already!"

He pointed to a sign hanging on the wall. It read *Zutritt verboten!* Leash approached to take a gander.

"They all look alike, Hitch."

"Sir, I'm telling you, we're lost!" Hitch shook his head. "It's a goddamn anthill! The deeper you go, the larger it gets!"

Leash glanced at him, worried. Hitch was getting edgy. Better keep him occupied.

"Why don't you make yourself useful and sniff out the rat hole up there?" Leash said, pointing to a niche in the wall twenty feet ahead.

Hitch grimaced and headed over. Leash looked at the sketched map.

"Krause's map says we're—"

"Sir, look at this!" Hitch yelled.

He stood before the niche in the wall, gazing into it with awestruck eyes. Leash and May rushed over.

The niche was an entrance. Behind it stretched an underground cavern, big as a factory hall. Its walls, carved out of permafrost, glistened in shades of blue. Scaffolding lined the walls along the perimeter. Long, industrial gantries hung suspended beneath the ceiling. A battery of klieg lights glared down from them, their beams trained on the center of the cavern like spotlights on a soundstage. Right there in the center, pinned down by the harsh light, hunched a wooden medieval house with a shingled roof. It looked completely out-of-place, almost surreal, as if someone had borrowed it from some ancient fairy tale and dropped it in the middle of Greenland. Carved on the transom was an inscription in the angelic alphabet. May's eyes widened with wonder.

"The Golden Chamber," she whispered.

Leash cocked his gun.

"Keep your eyes open."

Guns drawn, they stepped in. Their eyes keen on the surroundings, they marched across the cavern and approached the chamber. The front door stood wide open. Two small windows on either side stared at them like a pair of probing eyes. Guns leveled, Leash and Hitch peeked in through the door.

Inside was a large, dim room lit by flickering candles. The décor was eerie, almost unsettling. Mysterious inscriptions and sigils covered the timber walls like an occult wallpaper. Bookshelves bowed under the weight of ancient, crumbling manuscripts. The place looked like it held all the wisdom of the ages. In the back corner, half-hidden in shadows, stood an oversized clay figure of a man. They stepped warily into the chamber, eyes on the mysterious figure. May tiptoed over. The clay man had a sinister, rough-hewn face. His hollow eyes stared ahead with perfect indifference, as if he had nothing but contempt for the world. May ran her fingers across the clay face. Her touch was gentle, almost caressing.

Leash watched May. Her eyes burned with awe.

Stuck in the figure's mouth was a thin scroll of yellowed parchment. May cautiously plucked it out, her fingers trembling with excitement. Written on the scroll was a single, stark word in the angelic alphabet.

"The word of creation," she whispered.

A quiet voice came from a dark corner.

"May?"

Leash saw a silhouette lurking in the shadows. He spun around and leveled his flashlight.

An old man sat there in a wheelchair, shielding his eyes from the flashlight, a cane held out defensively in his hand. A frayed, woolen suit hung from his drooping shoulders. His eyes were ringed with insomnia, his horn-rim glasses broken on one side. A silly bow tie dangled under his chin. Leash nearly chuckled. A *bow tie* in Greenland?

May's arms shot up in joy.

"Dad!"

She dashed across the chamber and threw her arms around her father's neck. For a few awkward moments, Leash and Hitch watched the barrage of hugs and kisses. The professor gaped at May with disbelief.

"How did you . . ."

"With their help," she pointed to Leash and Hitch. Her voice was tinged with pride.

Leash waved a salute.

"Captain Leash, sir. U.S. Rangers."

The professor's face lit up with a smile. He nodded a "thank you." Leash harrumphed.

"Hate to interrupt, sir, but we need to find a way to knock out that ghost. Can you get working on this?"

May peeled herself off her father's chest and wheeled her father toward a nearby table.

"We've got the missing half of the psalm," she said.

From her dispatch bag May pulled out her half of the psalm and put it down on the table. The professor gave her a grim look.

"Albers took my half from me."

The news hit like a gavel. May gaped at her father, her face long with dejection.

"This can't be true . . ."

Professor Benedict flashed a triumphant smile. He held up his walking cane.

"But first I made a copy."

He unscrewed the brass knob off the top of his cane. From a hollow compartment inside he pulled out a rolled-up piece of paper. He straightened it out and put it down on the table. It was the other half of the psalm.

May sighed with relief.

"Thank heavens."

She leaned over the table and aligned the two pieces, edge to edge. Her gaze flitted across the verses.

"The words match," she smiled. "We've got the whole thing!"

She and her father pored over the psalm, engrossed by the riddle hidden within. Leash pointed to the door.

"We'll step outside to secure—"

He stopped mid-sentence. Neither May nor her dad were listening. Leash sighed and turned to Hitch.

"What I said."

He and Hitch stepped out and scanned the surroundings. The cavern stood silent and empty. Yawning in the walls around them were the openings of four access tunnels. Leash pointed them out to Hitch.

"Let's put up Christmas balls, just in case," Leash said. He pointed to the two tunnels on the left. "You take these two, I'll take the others."

They split up and headed into the tunnels.

Leash stretched a trip wire across the width of the tunnel. He pulled out a hand grenade and cautiously hung it on the wire by the pin. The grenade wobbled a bit. Leash carefully nudged it to a stop with his finger. He straightened up and gave the wire a satisfied look.

"Merry Christmas, everyone."

He headed off into the next tunnel.

Unseen by Leash, something or someone watched him closely from the dark void at the far end of the tunnel. Hidden in the shadows, something large and inhuman began to creep down the tunnel toward the cavern visible in the distance.

May and her father leaned over the psalm, their eyes burning in deep concentration. Their fingers ran fervently across the verses, as if the secret hidden within could be soaked up right through the fingertips.

"I read my half many times over but I couldn't find anything." May said.

"Neither could I in mine."

"It must be something they have in common. Something you see only if you put the two together."

Their eyes darted to and fro across the text, word to word, line to line . . .

The professor furrowed his brow. His eyes sparked with the flash of an insight.

"Look at the beginning and the end!"

He pointed out the beginning of the psalm:

Arca serenum me . . .

The end read:

. . . regem munere sacra.

May's gaze flitted anxiously between the two spots. "What about them?"

Professor Benedict grabbed a piece of paper and quickly copied over the beginning of the psalm: *Arca serenum me . . .*

"Look what you get when you spell the final verse backwards!"

Beneath the beginning of the psalm, he copied the end of the psalm backwards: *arca serenum me . . .*

"It's the same thing!" May's jaw dropped. "The whole psalm is a palindrome!"

Professor Benedict rubbed hard on his forehead.

"But what does it mean?"

May furrowed her brow. Her pupils jittered side to side, as if her frontal lobes were doing heavy lifting. Her gaze was so intense, it looked like her skull could blow up in a puff of hot steam at any moment. Then her face lit up with a divine epiphany.

"That's the answer!"

"What is?"

Without a word of explanation, May reached for the scroll from the clay man's mouth with the word of creation written across. She grasped a piece of paper and copied over the word backwards.

Her eyes burned bright.

"To shut down the Golem, you spell the word backwards!"

Professor Benedict gaped at her, astonished.

"How could something this simple elude me for months?"

He let out a heavy sigh. He reclined in his wheelchair and closed his eyes. His face took on the bleak grimace of a man about to write his last will.

"Finally, I'll get a chance to fix what I've done," he whispered.

"What do you mean, Dad?"

The professor opened his eyes and locked a somber gaze with May. He pointed to the manuscripts filling up the shelves.

"See all this? It's all about playing God, May. Scientists are thieves. We love to steal secrets from the Almighty. Like kids pinching cookies from the pantry."

He swung his arm around, pointing at the world at large.

"Remember why they built the Tower of Babel? To reach the heavens. Now we've got new Towers of Babel. They're called rockets."

May eyed him, bewildered.

"Dad, I don't understand—"

"I'll let you on a secret, May," the professor lowered his voice. "When the Germans kidnapped me, I resisted. They threatened me, so I started working. But then . . . I noticed that I worked hard even without their threats."

May gaped at her father in astonishment. His stare was blunt.

"May, I *wanted* to make the Golem! To beat all those who failed before me! Once you taste the powers of creation, they seduce you. You keep telling yourself that you'd be able to control them, that you'll use them for good, that—"

He stopped mid-sentence, too choked up to continue. May hugged him.

"Dad . . ." she struggled to find the right words, "Don't blame yourself for the sins of the world. That's God's job."

Silence fell on the chamber. May and her dad held each other in a tight embrace.

Leash and Hitch stepped in. Leash opened his mouth to say something. He hesitated, seeing May in her dad's arms. Should he wait? . . . There was no time to lose.

"Any luck?"

May and her father promptly peeled off each other, noticing they weren't alone. May showed Leash the backward-spelled word.

"Here's the silver bullet. If we could only shove it down his mouth—"

Bang! A distant blast cut her off. A crescendo of thudding footsteps followed. It sounded as if something massive were approaching the cavern.

They bolted out of the chamber.

"There!" Hitch pointed at an access tunnel.

The fiery blasts of grenade explosions billowed far inside the tunnel. Something else was in there, moving toward them. They couldn't quite make out the shape. Barely visible in the red glow of the blasts was a menacing, jagged silhouette. Whatever it was, it crept toward the hall.

"It's him!" Hitch yelled.

Bang! Bang!

More explosions rumbled in the distance, this time coming from the other access tunnels. Fear glinted in May's eyes.

"He's coming from all sides!"

"Damn, he got us cornered!" Hitch said.

Leash turned to Professor Benedict.

"Is there any other way out of here?"

The professor pointed off to the side, toward the cavern wall. "The elevator!"

Leash, May, and Hitch swiveled their heads in unison. Two steel rails of an industrial freight elevator ran up the height of the permafrost wall and vanished in a square hole in the ceiling, about 150 feet off the ground.

"Come on!" Leash yelled.

May gripped her father's wheelchair. They darted over . . .

The elevator was a car-sized platform surrounded on all sides by an open-top, chain-link cage. Leash gazed up. The rails ran up inside a square shaft dug out in permafrost. At the top of the shaft, 200 feet off the ground, a streak of light was seeping in through an open loading gate.

The thuds in the tunnels grew louder.

Hitch looked around, desperate. He spotted the elevator's controls. It was a brick-sized Bakelite box with three large buttons, hooked up to the motor with a thick cable. The buttons were labeled in German. Hitch eyed May.

"Which one opens the door?!"

May pointed to the button marked *Tür auf.* Hitch hit it. The cage door slid open with an electric hum.

A strange, pained look crept onto the professor's face. His eyes flitted rapidly between May and the access tunnels, as if he was weighing a fateful decision. A tear welled up in his eye. It looked like he was about to do something. Something very important . . .

May gripped his wheelchair, about to roll it into the elevator.

"No, you all go in first!" The professor shook his head. "There's a ledge in the loading gate up there. If I go first, I'll be blocking your way out!"

Leash nodded. He, May, and Hitch stepped into the elevator. Unseen by them, the professor quickly reached for the controls and hit a button. The door slid shut, locking the others inside. May whirled, her eyebrows shooting up in surprise. She gaped at her father through the chain-link cage.

"Dad, what are you doing?!"

The professor hit another button. The elevator jerked, moaned, and began to lift off the ground. The professor locked a tearful gaze with May.

"You wouldn't make it far with me in a wheelchair, May. I'll slow him down. You'll make it out of here."

May rattled the cage like a trapped beast.

"No, Dad, please!"

Seen from the ascending elevator, the professor's figure shrank with each second.

"Good bye, May," he said. "I must face what I've unleashed."

All of a sudden, a huge shadow fell on him. May, Leash, and Hitch glanced up. Their eyes bugged out.

The Golem's limbs crawled out separately from several access tunnels, like severed sections of a mammoth earthworm. The parts quickly fused together and shot up to form a thirty-foot tall leviathan with long, arching limbs made of ice blocks and parts of German vehicles. Its shape was malformed and crooked, like a nightmarish cross between a hunchback and a praying mantis. The Golem was bigger than ever.

The professor spun his wheelchair to face the monster. The Golem stood still, staring at him, as if surprised to see an old man trying to confront him. Face red with effort, the professor braced himself and slowly rose up from his wheelchair. His quivering hand on the cane, he made a few feeble steps toward the Golem. He halted a few yards from the Golem's limb and gazed up. *Way* up. The Golem stared back down at him. The frail human and the monster locked a hopelessly unmatched gaze. The professor's voice quivered, but his words were firm.

"I made you."

The faceless monster watched him with cold indifference. Perhaps he understood what the man was saying. Perhaps the old man was just a petty nuisance. The Golem swiveled his head and looked around. A ten-foot long iron pipe lay nearby. In an instant the pipe heaved off the ground and sailed through the air toward the Golem's arm. The Golem grasped it and leaned on it like a cane. His arm trembled, mimicking the professor's posture. The two faced each other like a distorted mirror image in an outlandish fun house. The professor frowned in anger.

"Are you mocking me, you wretch?!"

There was no reply. All of a sudden, the Golem gripped the pipe firmly and swung it like a baseball bat. A horrid swish cut through the air.

May cried out.

"Dad!"

Leash quickly hugged her, shielding her from the grisly sight below.

The professor's horn-rim glasses hit the ground, shattered and sprayed with blood.

Hearing May's scream, the Golem gazed up toward the elevator. He hurried over, gripped the elevator rails, and began to climb up in pursuit.

Horror in their eyes, Leash and the others watched it all from the elevator cage. Leash glanced up. The loading gate at the top of the shaft was only ten feet away.

"We're close! Give him hell!"

He and Hitch cocked their guns and blasted a punishing salvo straight down into the metal plate of the floor. The plate sizzled with sparks; the bullets ripped right through.

The Golem climbed up the rails, undeterred, his gaze on the elevator. The hail of bullets from above tore through his limbs, ice shards spraying. It didn't matter in the least. The Golem crept closer and closer, like a mammoth panther stalking its prey. When he was only a few yards away, his arm shot up and grasped the elevator.

Wham! The elevator jolted, the platform tilted askew. Leash and the others reeled over, barely able to keep their balance. The engine howled to high heavens, stalled against the Golem's grip.

Leash glanced up in despair. The loading bay was only a few feet away. A quick decision flashed in his eyes. He cradled his hands and turned to May.

"Get up there!"

Using Leash's hands for footing, May climbed out of the elevator cage into the loading gate above. The elevator jolted again; the Golem firmed his grip on the platform. Hitch spun and let loose a furious blast into the arm holding the elevator.

"Take this, you beast!"

The bullets shredded the icy fingers like a thousand vicious ice picks. No dice. The shattered fingers grew back like the heads of a Hydra. Hitch looked at Leash, desperate.

"He ain't letting go!"

They were down to their last seconds. Hitch's eyes sparked with determination. He cradled his hands and turned to Leash.

"Get up, sir! You can pull me up from above!"

Leash climbed out of the cage using Hitch's hands for footing and slipped into the loading gate above.

The Golem gripped the platform with another arm. The elevator dropped a few feet with a horrid squeal.

Leash and May lay prone in the loading bay, holding out their arms down into the elevator shaft, toward Hitch.

"Give me your hand, Hitch!" Leash yelled.

Hitch stood up on his toes and stretched out his arm as far has he could. No cigar. He was short by a few inches.

"Come on, Hitch!"

Hitch strained for one more desperate try . . .

Crrrack!

The Golem pulled hard on the elevator. The elevator jolted, screeched like a slaughtered pig, and dropped down a few more feet, the floor bent like origami. Hitch looked up. Leash's hand slipped far out of his grasp.

Hitch clenched his jaws with the grim look of a man who knows he's a goner. He pulled out the photo of his daughter, kissed it, and looked at Leash with the tragic stare of a man writing a suicide note.

"Here's my pardon."

He raised his gun up and trained it at the pulleys holding the elevator.

Leash's eyes bugged out.

"Hitch!"

Hitch blasted away. The pulleys shattered to pieces. The elevator cables snapped in half, and whipped around like rabid snakes.

His mouth open in shock, Leash watched on as the elevator plummeted down, taking the Golem and Hitch with it.

CHAPTER X

THE LOADING BAY was a large, industrial hall with
two cargo ramps stretched out in the center. Rows of bare
bulbs hung overhead, casting dirty, yellow light against
the grimy walls. Yawning in the middle of the floor was
the square well of the elevator shaft.

Leash stood by the window, peering out through
his binoculars. Before him sprawled the badlands of
the frozen bay, all covered with jutting pressure plates
like a golf course from hell. On the far, northern shore
stretched the flat belt of the airstrip, lined with hangars
and signal sleeves.

"We gotta get to the airstrip," Leash said.

The echo of his words was his only reply. Leash turned
around and gazed toward the other side of the hall. May
sat there on the floor, back against the wall, teary-eyed,
face buried in dejection. She paid no heed.

Leash watched her for a moment. It didn't take a
psychologist to figure out what was wrong. His voice
ratcheted down to a soft whisper.

"Your father did what he had to do."

May sat silent. Leash shuffled over and crouched next
to her, his head level with May's.

"We can't bring him back," he said. "But if we pull this off, we'll do what he'd have wished."

May remained silent.

"I, too, lost someone I loved," Leash said. He took a deep breath. "My wife."

May eyed him through her tears.

"She left me," Leash said.

"Why?"

"I resented her love."

May eyed him, baffled, "I don't understand."

Leash lowered his voice.

"I'm sure Hitch told you about my mother."

May opened her mouth, about to protest—

"No point denying," Leash hushed her. "I know he tells everyone."

May watched him in silence. He sat down on the floor next to her and stared off.

"You see, when you give someone the power to love you, you give them the power to hurt you. I didn't want to be hurt again. So I gave my wife nothing but suspicion. Always looking out for how she could hurt me. I treated her as if she had already betrayed me. One day she got fed up and—"

May listened intently, her eyes on Leash.

"Some people leave you 'cause you keep fighting with *them*." He sighed. "Others leave you 'cause you keep fighting with *yourself*."

For a moment, they sat in silence. May slowly reached over and touched Leash's hand. Leash returned the touch. Their fingertips clung together they way charged amber draws a feather.

Whack!

Something hit the floor near the entrance. Leash leapt to his feet, gun trained. A man clambered into the hall, knocking over a stack of crates. He staggered toward Leash and May with a drunken, limping gait. Leash knew that limp too well. He squinted at the man, surprised.

"Slocombe?"

"Cap-cappptain . . ."

The medic's speech was slurred, his eyes glazed over with dementia. Leash sighed. *Morphine.*

"How did you get out?" he said.

"I was in the basement . . . performing a . . . medical . . . procedure . . ."

"On your veins?"

"I . . . no, sir . . . you see . . . I was in pain . . . I fled through the window . . . cut my arm on the glass . . ."

He showed Leash a slash on the sleeve of his parka.

"It was horrible, Captain . . . horrible . . ."

"Did anyone else make it?"

"No, sir," Slocombe shook his head. "But I found a way out of here . . . came back to get you . . . you see, there's a snow jeep in the warehouse . . . can get us out . . ."

"What warehouse?"

Slocombe pointed out the window. A dingy, long structure loomed about a hundred yards away. Leash stared at Slocombe, hesitating. How much could he trust this junkie?

"You're sure about it?"

Slocombe nodded eagerly.

"I even brought the keys."

He handed Leash a set of heavy-duty car keys. They were marked with German army insignia and the word *Kübelwagen.*

Leash stretched out his hand toward May. "Come on." He helped her to her feet.

A few German vehicles lurked behind a snow mound, like a wolf pack stalking its prey. Albers sat behind the wheel in an open-top jeep. Ramsey, seated next to him, peered nervously through his binoculars toward the loading bay two hundred yards ahead.

"You sure it's going to work?"

Albers nodded calmly.

Leash, May, and Slocombe slunk down the main aisle of a vast warehouse. The place was dark; faint light filtered down through the skylights. Murky side aisles branched off left and right, each flanked by towering racks with industrial supplies.

"Where is it?" Leash eyed Slocombe.

Slocombe led them into one of the side aisles. A vehicle hunched there, covered by a tarp. Leash lifted the tarp. It was a *Kübelwagen*, a sturdy, open-top German jeep. Leash checked the wheels. Big, spiky, snow tires. Leash nodded, satisfied.

He looked around. Stacked next to the jeep were wooden crates labeled *Munition*. Leash lifted the lid off a crate. Inside was a batch of hand grenades, tucked in wood shavings like eggs in a basket. Leash turned to Slocombe and May.

"Give me a hand."

They picked up the crate with grenades and put it in the jeep's cargo bed. Leash kept rummaging through the ammo supplies. A long, coffin-sized crate lay off to the side, labeled *Vorsicht! Versuchsmodell!*

"What does it say?" Leash pointed it out to May.

"Caution: prototype!"

He opened it up and whistled. Tucked inside was a bazooka-like *Panzerfaust* tipped with a bulky warhead. He picked it up and eyed it intently. This could be a . . .

He spun toward May, pointing at the warhead.

"Write the magic word here."

May gave him a surprised look.

"Just do it," he said.

May pulled out her lipstick and scribbled the creation word backwards on the warhead.

"That's what I call a kiss of death," Leash eyed the warhead with satisfaction. He set down the *Panzerfaust* on the jeep's cargo bed.

"Assuming we have a fighting chance," May said, a somber look on her face.

"How do you mean?"

"The Golem has killed his maker. He'll grow bigger than ever."

Leash sighed.

"Can't say we've got a choice. All right, let's—" he frowned and look around. "Where's Slocombe?"

They heard footsteps near the entrance gate. *Many* footsteps. Fear in their eyes, Leash and May peeked out from behind a rack. A few men stood in the gate, visible in grim, backlit silhouettes. It was Albers, Ramsey, and a few SS men, guns at the ready. Slocombe, half-delirious, leaned against the wall nearby.

"Your men are easily bought, Captain Leash," Albers yelled toward the dark aisles. He reached into Slocombe's pocket and pulled out a fistful of morphine vials.

"I . . . I'm sorry, Captain . . . I had to . . . I needed to . . ." Slocombe's slurred words were barely audible.

Leash clenched his teeth. "Damn idiot."

Albers smashed the vials on the floor, contempt in his eyes. Slocombe's eyes opened wide in horror.

"Nooo!" He dived onto the floor and greedily swept together the drug, the way a starving man collects his last bread crumbs. Albers pulled out his pistol.

Bang!

He shot Slocombe dead.

Leash and May quickly backed into their aisle.

Albers scanned the warehouse. He couldn't see much in the dark. He spied a bank of light switches on the wall. He flicked switch No. 1. Aisle 1 lit up. He flicked the next switch . . .

Leash glanced off to the side, concern in his eyes. The nearby aisles were lighting up, one by one, closer and closer.

"Get in!" he turned to May. "I'll be right back!"

May jumped into the jeep. Leash vanished in the nearby aisle.

Albers flicked the switch No. 6. Aisle 6 lit up. A car-sized shadow jutted out from inside.

"Gotcha."

The Germans sneaked down the main aisle toward the shadow, guns drawn.

Leash returned and quietly climbed into the jeep. May eyed him quizzically, but Leash shushed her.

Albers and his men peeked into Aisle 6. A car-sized object stood in its center, covered by a tarp. Guns trained, they sneaked into the aisle and closed in on the object. Albers signaled one of his men. The man tiptoed over to the object and grasped a corner of the tarp. Albers nodded. The SS man yanked the tarp off. The SS men blasted a furious salvo into the target and . . .

"Hold it!" Albers yelled, anger in his eyes.

The Germans ceased fire. They were shooting at a stack of empty carton boxes.

Ramsey frowned, "What the—"

All of a sudden, the *Kübelwagen* roared out of the next aisle and zoomed past the Germans toward the entrance gate.

"*Verdammt!*" Albers yelled.

The jeep bolted out of the warehouse like a racehorse. A few seconds later, the Germans darted out in pursuit. Albers watched the jeep. It was speeding off fast.

"Come on!" he yelled. "He's getting away!"

The Germans rushed toward a nearby snow mound. Hidden behind it were their vehicles: a few jeeps and half-track with a flak cannon manned by two gunners.

Leash clawed the steering wheel; the jeep highballed straight toward the bay shore. The sloping embankment was only yards away.

"Hold on!" he yelled.

May gripped her seat. The jeep dived down the slope and hit the frozen bay, bouncing on the bumps like a toy car. Fridge-sized ice plates towered all around them. Leash swerved left and right to dodge them.

A choir of diesel engines roared from behind. Leash and May turned around. The German vehicles were charging in pursuit.

An unearthly phenomenon was taking place in the base. Tanks and trucks dragged across the roads by themselves, in an eerie, ghostly parade. Whole building sections broke off by themselves and sailed through the air, propelled by an unseen force. All of this matter, tons and tons of it, was converging onto a single location . . .

The jeep was halfway across the bay; the north shore just half a mile off. Leash gave the jeep a worried glance. The poor thing creaked like a wooden rickshaw as it barreled over the bumps. Leash had this nagging feeling it would fall apart any moment.

"Let's pray this jerry-rig can take the ride!"

May swiveled her head, her eyes wide in fear.

"They're after us!"

Leash turned around. Albers tore in pursuit like a locomotive. Leash stomped on the gas.

A huge shadow moved across the base. Something of mammoth proportions was rising above the buildings. Giant limbs made of bunched-up tanks stomped down a snow-swept road, each footstep an earth-shaking tremor. Whatever it was, it was headed for the bay.

Albers put on a smug grin. They were closing in on Leash. The jeep scurried away before them like a rat on a sinking ship. Albers reached for his radio.

"Give them a nudge!"

A German gunner on the half-track jammed a shell up the breech. He trained the cannon at the jeep and . . .

Wham!

The blast tore a hole in the ice, ten yards from the jeep, spewing out a column of water.

"Reload!" Albers yelled.

Leash and May traded frightened looks. Leash glanced back at the cargo bed.

"Grenades!"

May quickly picked up a grenade. She eyed it with bewilderment.

"What do I do?!"

"Rip off the pin and toss'em out!"

"Do I count off?!"

"Yes!" Leash rolled his eyes. "To *one!*"

May ripped off the pin and lobbed the grenade toward the Germans.

Blam!

A spray of water shot up in the air, twenty feet before Albers's jeep. Albers swerved hard to get out of harm's way. The smirk vanished from his face. He firmed the grip on his radio.

"Fire!"

The flak cannon blasted again. This time the shell missed Leash's jeep by only a few feet. The ice split open, cracks tearing under the jeep like demon claws. Leash veered off. The jeep bounced hard, the rear wheels hitting the edge of the crack. They barely stayed afloat.

Leash clenched his teeth. "We won't stand this for much longer!"

Albers beamed, his mouth tight against the radio.

"He's breaking up! One more!"

All of a sudden, a huge shadow fell onto the bay, dimming all light like a skyscraper. May glanced over toward the base. She looked up . . . and up . . . and up . . . Her eyes bugged out.

"Holy heavens!"

The German gunner froze, a cannon shell in his hands. He stared toward the base, wide-eyed, a frightened whisper on his lips.

"*Mein Gott . . .*"

Albers and Ramsey followed his gaze.

On the bay shore stood a giant. The Golem was now a three hundred-foot tall Goliath made of whole vehicles, parts of buildings, and steel framework. His monstrous limbs spanned the shoreline like a suspension bridge from hell. Nazi markings on the vehicles dotted his entire body, as if the spirit of Nuremberg rallies had turned to flesh and come to life in this behemoth.

What stood there was evil incarnate.

The Golem swiveled his head to scan the bay. Far beneath him, scattered like toys, were Leash's jeep and the Germans' trucks. The jeep drew his instant attention. He lumbered toward the bay, his feet thudding against the ground. He stepped down into the frozen bay, his giant legs tearing through the ice like butter. He charged straight toward the jeep.

Leash saw it.

"Christ, he's after us!" he yelled.

The Germans watched the Golem, slack-jawed. Albers squinted to judge the Golem's direction.

"He wants Leash," he said to Ramsey.

The German gunner didn't hear him. Panic-eyed, he gaped at the oncoming Golem. The monster charged across the bay like a steamroller.

"He's coming this way!" the gunner yelled to his comrade, "Knock him off his feet!"

He shoved the shell up the breech, trained the cannon at the Golem, and fired away.

Wham!

The salvo hit one of the Golem's legs. The hardware that made up the leg shattered in a shower of iron debris. The Golem leaned sideways under his own weight.

A gleam of triumph flashed in the gunner's eyes.

But then . . . The debris from the Golem's leg pulled itself back together and reformed into its previous shape. The Golem marched on.

Undeterred. Unstoppable. Unmoved.

The gleam of triumph died cold in the gunner's eyes, replaced by mortal fear.

"Cease fire, you idiots! He's not after us!" Albers barked into his radio.

The gunner paid no heed, deafened by panic.

"One more time!" he yelled to his comrade.

He dropped another shell into the breech and let loose. The salvo hit another leg. The monster sank momentarily under his own weight, then rose again, as strong as ever. But this time his stare shifted from Leash's jeep to the Germans. He looked angered by the nuisance, the way a man looks at a lap dog biting his leg. He changed course and started toward the Germans.

"For God's sake, cease fire!" Albers screamed his lungs out into the radio, veins bulging on his face. "You're drawing his attention!"

May and Leash watched it all from their jeep. Leash saw it right away: the Golem had changed his mind, if only for a moment. Leash firmed his grip on the wheel.

"They got his attention!" he yelled. "Let's get the hell out of here!"

He floored the gas. They zoomed off toward the north shore.

Albers and Ramsey watched bug-eyed as the Golem strode closer and closer. It seemed like his mammoth scale had slowed down time, each second now an eternity.

Albers was pale like zinc, a deadly fear in his eyes. *"Mein Gott . . ."*

He stomped on the brakes. Their jeep skidded in a wide arc. The inertia flung Albers out of the cabin. He hit the ground and rolled over. Had he landed on ice he'd have broken all bones, but a layer of snow cushioned the blow. He swallowed the pain, climbed to his feet, and hurried off toward the shore.

Ramsey wrestled with the steering wheel to control the skidding jeep.

The Golem halted in front of the Germans, legs spread a hundred yards apart like the Colossus of Rhodes. For a moment he gazed down at the tiny vehicles at his feet. Then he then hauled off and brought down his arm in a giant, sweeping arc . . .

Ramsey looked up. His eyes bugged out. Coming down at him was an instant death. It was the last thing he ever saw.

Ice and water shot up in massive columns, as the Golem pounded on the Germans, hammering them down into the frozen bay.

Leash's jeep tore away like there was no tomorrow. May looked back, unable to keep her eyes off the mayhem. "My God . . ."

The frightful spectacle was in full swing. Blow after blow, the Golem smashed the Germans into oblivion, like an angry boy sinking toy boats in a bathtub.

Leash and May reached the north shore, their battered jeep struggling uphill. The engine dripped oil, the hood steamed like a boiler, the chassis was coming apart at the seams. Leash rose in his seat and looked around. Straight ahead, about a hundred yards away, stretched the flattened swath of the airstrip. The hill range loomed right behind it. Closer to the right stood a small wooden tool shed. An access road ran off to the left, lined on both sides by a cluster of grimy warehouses. Leash frowned, working out a plan of action. If he could only lure the monster away . . . Yeah, this could work.

He pulled over by the shed and gave May a determined stare.

"Wait here!"

"What about you?!"

"I'll catch up! Go!"

May jumped out of the jeep and hid behind the tool shed. Leash jammed on the gas and zoomed off down the access road.

The Golem was completing his work of destruction. He heaved the wreck of Ramsey's jeep, crumpled it like paper, and hurled it aside. The wreck plowed into the ice plates on the bay and shattered to pieces.

The nuisance was gone.

The Golem swiveled his head and scanned the bay. Far in the distance, the dark speck of Leash's jeep zipped across the north shore. The Golem hurried over.

Leash clutched the wheel, his foot jammed on the gas, his face tense like a drum skin. The jeep whooshed down the access road, kicking up a plume of snow.

Leash turned around and scanned the cargo bed. There it was: a shovel. He propped it between his seat and the gas pedal. It worked. The shovel was stuck, pushing on the pedal. The jeep now drove on its own. Leash dropped his helmet on top of the shovel handle and gave it an appraising look. Nice. Would pass for a driver from a distance. He looked back.

The Golem steamed through the bay like a bulldozer, his gaze on the jeep. He was about to reach the shore.

Leash checked the road up ahead: a straight, long stretch. Just what he needed. He grabbed the *Panzerfaust* from the cargo bed and jumped out.

Plop! He hit a roadside snow pile, rolled over a few times, and promptly buried himself in a snow mound behind a warehouse. He gazed up, eyes wide.

The Golem stepped ashore with an earth-shaking thump and strode on, his limbs ripping through warehouses like a tornado. Leash ducked and covered his head. The ground shook like a fault line. A hail of debris from the torn buildings showered on Leash in the Golem's wake.

The worst was over; the monster had passed by. Leash leapt to his feet and sprinted off the other way.

The jeep zipped down the road like a runaway train. The Golem was steaming in pursuit.

Somewhere along the north shore, Albers clambered up the embankment. He was bruised and battered, but his eyes glared with determination. He surveyed the surroundings. About fifty yards ahead, a lone hangar stood by the airstrip. Albers hurried over.

May huddled behind the wooden tool shed, her teeth chattering fast and loud. She herself couldn't tell if that was cold or fear. Maybe both.

Someone gripped her by the arm.

"You're okay?"

May whirled, startled. It was Leash, panting, his face red from effort, the *Panzerfaust* flung over his shoulder. May looked at him with concern.

"I was so worried! I saw him pass—"

"I'm fine," he shushed her with a sweep of his hand and glanced anxiously toward the Golem. "We better get out of here before he catches on." He took her by the elbow. "Come on!"

They sprinted off toward the hangars.

The runaway jeep whizzed down the road. Leash's helmet wobbled on the shovel like an epileptic. All of a sudden, the jeep hit a bump. It arced through the air, hit the ground, rolled over, and plowed into a big snow mound, upside down. The engine snorted and died. The wheels kept spinning idly.

The Golem was closing in fast.

Leash and May crouched behind the hangar. They peeked out from behind the corner. No one was in sight. Backs to the wall, they sneaked toward the open gate. When they were just a few feet away, Leash waved May to stop. May gave him a questioning glance. Leash pointed to a gun barrel sticking out of the gate at chest level.

Leash gingerly tiptoed toward the gate. When he was three feet away, he grabbed the barrel, pushed it down, and quickly aimed his own gun at whoever was behind the gate. It was a German pilot in a winter parka. The man was so startled, his arms went up without a single word from Leash.

"*Nicht schiessen!*"

"Shut up."

Holding his gun on the German, Leash peeked in. The hangar was a dark, grimy hall, its corners littered with gas canisters and airplane parts. In the middle hunched a German ski plane in polar camouflage, its cargo door wide open. Leash crouched down and warily scanned the hangar floor behind the plane. There was no one in sight. He got up and fixed the pilot with a probing stare.

"You're alone?"

The pilot nodded eagerly. Leash held his stare on the man for a moment. It didn't look like he was lying, but you never know . . .

Leash waved his gun, pointing at the plane.

"Get in!"

The pilot hurried over and climbed into the cabin. Leash and May followed him onboard. Leash took the seat right next to the pilot and waved his gun at him.

"Start the plane!"

His hands trembling, the pilot set the throttle to *Start* and turned the ignition switch. The propeller twitched a quarter of a turn. The engine snorted like a clogged drain and died. The pilot set the mixture to *Max* and tried again. The propellers twitched again and . . .

Vroooom! The engine sprang to life with a healthy rumble. The pilot revved it up.

The Golem reached the upturned jeep. He nudged the jeep with his limb to turn it over. The jeep turned over . . . *empty.* A lone helmet rolled out onto the snow. The Golem stared long and hard at it, as if riled by the nasty surprise.

An engine buzzed in the distance. The Golem swiveled his head. Far on the north shore, a ski plane bolted out of a hangar and taxied onto the airstrip. It made a quick U-turn and took position at the start of the runway.

The tons of hardware in the Golem's body pulled taut with a horrid, angry squeal. The monster dashed toward the airstrip, the ground quaking under his limbs.

Leash looked out the plane's windshield. The mountains loomed large in the distance, enclosing the airstrip on the other end.

"Get us out of here!" he yelled at the pilot, "We gotta clear the hills!"

The pilot gunned the throttle. The engines howled, ready for action. The plane lunged forth and sped up down the runway, trailing a rooster tail of snow.

They were three-quarters down the runway when the plane reached the climb speed. The landing gear began to lift off the ground. All of a sudden, a mountain-sized shadow fell on the plane. May turned around. Her eyes bugged out.

"Jesus Christ . . ."

Leash turned around.

The Golem was after them. He no longer *moved* through the surroundings. He *ate* the surroundings. He was a raging force of nature, plowing through the base like a mobile volcano, sucking in every atom of matter in its path. Whole buildings shot up in the air, blown up from their foundations, only to be absorbed into one, compact mass. The Golem was controlling matter on a titanic scale. He was closing in fast, like a lion going for the kill.

"Get us up, now!" Leash yelled to the pilot.

The pilot yanked on the control stick, his hands shaking with fear. The plane pitched up and soared off the ground. Leash handed May the pilot's gun.

"Hold it!"

May grabbed the gun and aimed it at the pilot.

His *Panzerfaust* in hand, Leash backed into the cargo hold and looked around. A stack of wooden crates rose in the back. In the center, opposite the side door, stood a vertical pole bolted to the floor and the ceiling. Leash hurried over and gripped the pole to test it. It held firm. Leash turned to face the door, his back to the pole. He removed his belt and lashed himself to the pole, like Ulysses to the ship's mast.

May watched the Golem wide-eyed. The colossus was just seconds away from reaching the plane.

"Hurry up! He's right on us!" she yelled.

The plane was 500 feet off the ground when the Golem caught up with it. He raised one of his limbs, the size of the Brooklyn Bridge. Had it not been for the giant scale, he'd have looked like a man about to swat a fly.

May saw it. Her eyes popped out.

"Watch out!" she screamed to the pilot.

The pilot rolled left into a tight bank to get out of harm's way. May clutched her seat, fighting to keep her balance. The Golem's giant arm swished by like a plummeting Zeppelin. It missed the fuselage by a few yards. The trailing wake of turbulence caught the plane and sent it reeling. A piece of debris fell off the Golem's arm and hit a fuel tank under the wing. The tank broke up, spraying like a garden hose.

The pilot fought with the control stick, desperate to keep the plane level. He spied the fuel gauge. It dropped fast.

"We're losing fuel!"

"Do something!" May shouted toward Leash, "We can't take any more!"

"I'm on it!" he yelled back.

He checked the *Panzerfaust*: the inscribed warhead sat firmly in the barrel. He raised the rear sights and flicked the safety switch. All ready to go. All of a sudden, he caught a quick glimpse of two eyes glaring from behind the crates in the back. He spun around to face them. Their eyes met for a tense second . . .

Albers.

Leash reached for his gun. Too late. Albers lunged toward him and gripped his wrist, trying to get ahold of his gun. Leash fought back tooth and claw. They wrestled in tight quarters, teeth clenched, faces red with bulging veins. Leash's mind raced in overdrive. His odds were slim and getting slimmer. If only he weren't tied to the damn pole . . . Out of the corner of his eye, Leash spied the hinges of the cargo door just behind Albers. His eyes narrowed to two vicious slits. He knew what to do. He mustered up enough strength to fight Albers's grip and train his gun at the hinges. He blasted away.

The bullets ripped the hinges to shreds; the cargo door fell off. The plane lurched and wobbled as a gust of wind whooshed in, snowflakes swirling.

Albers turned around, eyes wide in fear. The door yawned open just behind him. Leash braced himself against the pole and kicked Albers with both feet. Albers flailed his arms, losing balance. He keeled backward and fell out of the plane, screaming his lungs out. His scream soon faded out, drowned by the howling winds.

A grin of triumph crossed through Leash's face. It vanished as soon as it appeared. One of the engines choked, sputtered in a grim staccato, and gave its last gasp.

The pilot pushed in the throttle. The remaining engine howled feebly. The plane didn't rise an inch.

"We've got no lift!"

Panic-eyed, May looked out the windshield.

The mountains loomed ahead, their peaks a few yards above the plane's level.

"We won't clear the hills!"

Out of the corner of her eye, she saw the Golem swing his arm again.

"Watch out!"

The pilot swerved right to dodge the blow.

May looked out the windshield. The mountains were too close for another maneuver.

"We can't hold him back!"

Leash flung the *Panzerfaust* over his shoulder and aimed it through the open door. He could see the Golem's head, but the monster faced the other way.

"Turn around!" Leash yelled toward the cabin.

His voice drowned in the howl of the wind.

"What?!" May shouted back.

"Fly by his head!" Leash screamed at the top of his lungs. "I need a good shot!"

The plane rolled left and headed straight toward the Golem. The Golem saw it. He raised his arm one more time. The plane was now at his mercy. This time there would be no missing.

Leash peered through the *Panzerfaust*'s sights, his finger hugging the trigger. The Golem still faced away. Leash gritted his teeth.

"Look at me, you damn beast!"

The Golem slowly swiveled toward the plane, as he brought his arm down to deliver the final blow.

May looked through the windshield. The Golem's giant head was right before her.

"God, he's right on us!"

Then it happened. Fate gave Leash a chance. The Golem's mouth, or what could pass for it, moved into his sights. Leash squinted like a hunter before the kill.

"Gotcha."

He pulled the trigger. The cargo hold lit up with the fiery blaze of the backblast. The warhead shot toward the Golem, trailing a plume of vapor. Time slowed down like molasses, one second stretched to eternity . . .

Bull's-eye.

The warhead hit the Golem's mouth.

The monster's arm froze mid-air. A short, violent jolt rippled along his limbs, as if someone had sent a billion volts through his body. For a moment, the Golem remained on his feet, his dark, monstrous silhouette against the blue horizon. Then his lower limbs collapsed. He slumped to his knees, the steel debris in his body grating horribly.

A deafening, dissonant screech pierced the air—the howl of a thousand dying gods. In a final gesture, the Golem held out his arm toward the sun behind the horizon, as if trying to hold on to life. He then leaned backwards and collapsed piece by piece in a majestic slow motion, like a demolished high-rise.

His mammoth body fell backward across the whole base in a Christ-like shape of a man with arms held out. The tons of debris that made up his body showered down, hitting the fuel silos. The silos exploded in billowing, orange fireballs, turning the base into a raging inferno.

The Golem ceased to be.

Deep down in the underground bunkers, the Golden Chamber was going through an eerie transformation. Strange, occult formulas and sigils were showing up on the walls, written by an invisible hand. The symbols began to smolder. Flames burst out of them as if a hellish breath blew through the chamber's walls. The whole chamber was now on fire. The wooden beams holding up the ceiling fell down, consumed by flames.

The vault of the underground cavern collapsed and buried the Golden Chamber in an avalanche of permafrost.

Leash and May gaped in awe at the destruction below. They sighed with relief, but their joy was short-lived. May glanced out the windshield. Her eyes bugged out.

"Watch out!"

The mountain ridge was only a few yards away. Rocky outcrops jutted out like claws, about to tear the plane to pieces.

The pilot's face swelled with blood, as he tugged on the control stick to pitch the plane . . .

Thwack!

The plane flew just above the ridge, grazing the outcrops with its soft belly. The rocks tore the landing gear right off. The cabin jolted, the pilot keeled over and lost control. They tumbled inside the plane like potatoes in a sack.

"God!" May screamed her lungs out.

The thump of the crash drowned her scream. The plane nose-dived, plunged into the snowy hillside on the other side, bounced a few times, and slid downhill until it finally came to a halt down at the foothills. The snowdrifts slowly settled down around it.

It soon got quiet. *Real* quiet.

The pilot and May lay motionless in the cabin, bloodied and bruised. Leash's body hung slumped, still tied to the pole.

A long silence followed.

CHAPTER XI

Leash was coming to. His mind was slowly return-
ing from some distant dimension, as if he'd just woken
up from ten years of coma. He slowly opened his eyes
and looked around. He didn't have the faintest idea how
much time had passed. A cold wind whizzed in through
the open cargo door. The plane was half-buried in snow.
He tried to move and . . .

Ouch! He hissed in pain. It felt like someone had
dumped a ton of hot bricks on his loins. He couldn't move
at all. *Damn.* His back must have taken a solid licking.

He tried to speak up and . . . Nothing. Nothing at all.
His throat was a lump of clay. Things didn't look too rosy.
Then he frowned and listened. He heard some strange
voices. There. He heard them again. *Americans.* Was this
real? A hallucination? A strange ringing in his ears? He
couldn't quite tell. The man's voice was coming from a
stone's throw outside the plane.

"All right, you Krauts, come on out, hands in the air.
Hände hoch, verstehen?"

A sense of reality was kicking in. Wait a second . . .
Those damn grunts outside had no idea who was inside

the German plane. Leash had to act fast. He opened his mouth. His throat squeaked feebly.

"I'm an . . . American . . ."

No cigar. He knew full well no one outside could hear his whimper. The voice outside was insistent.

"Come on out right now or we'll rip the damn plane to shreds! You've got ten seconds, Fritz! Ten . . . nine . . . eight . . ."

Leash looked around, desperate. He noticed the unit badge on his parka, dangling, nearly torn-off. With all the effort he could muster, he moved his arm and ripped it off. His face squirmed in pain as he managed to toss it out the window . . .

The badge landed in the snow. Someone in combat boots gingerly tiptoed over it to take a gander. The man was a U.S. soldier in a winter parka, Tommy gun in his hand. He leaned over, inspected the badge, and yelled to someone behind him.

"Sir, we found them!"

A choir of invisible voices repeated the words as if the message was being passed down a file.

"We found them!"

"We found them!"

Seen from high up, the scene looked like a game staged with toy soldiers. The crashed German plane lay half-buried in snowdrifts at the foothills, surrounded by a dozen U.S. soldiers in winter gear. They stood at the edge of a makeshift airstrip. An Air Force rescue plane crouched on the strip, its engines whirring with a gentle buzz.

Leash couldn't see any of it. His eyes glazed over; his arms slumped. The world spun all around him. Everything went black.

❋ ❋ ❋

The world was waking up from the polar night. The skies blossomed into a deep shade of blue. The yellow disc of the sun bounced above the horizon, braving the winds. The polar dawn broke out.

A small speck plodded across the empty sky: a lone transport plane.

Patches of sunlight sprinkled the cargo hold, its ribbed walls vibrating with the drone of the engines. Medical equipment lined the aisle on one side, a row of cot beds on the other. Leash slept on a bed, head buried deep under a tower of bandages. He was bruised all over, but his breath was even and calm. His eyes flitted under his eyelids. He was dreaming, a woman's face fading in and out before his mind's eye.

A patch of sunlight grazed his face. Leash opened his eyes, his eyelids fighting the sun. Half awake, he pondered the strange sight. The face in his dream had magically transformed. Leaning now over him was May, backlit by sunlight into a dreamy blur. With a turban of bandages on her head, she looked like an Arab princess.

Leash tried hard to gather his thoughts. He couldn't remember a thing. Was this face a reality? A dream? A strange, kitschy painting?

"Are you okay?" May smiled.

"Did I make it to heaven?"

He was dead serious. For all he knew, heaven could really look like a kitschy painting. He'd never been there.

May offered him coffee.

"Halfway."

Leash took an eager sip. Now he knew for sure he was still alive. No way coffee in heaven could have that roasty tang.

"How's your head?" May said.

Leash touched his bandages.

"There's a guy with a jackhammer in there. He's digging the Holland Tunnel."

Sunlight grazed Leash's eyes again. He squinted away, surprised to see the daylight.

"The sun came out," May smiled. "It's the polar dawn."

Leash frowned. Wait a second . . . *Polar dawn? . . . Polar? . . . Greenland?* . . . His mind was racing, the memories of the last few days falling back in place like pieces of a puzzle. He remembered now.

"What about the base?" he said.

"They couldn't even find it."

Leash gave her a questioning glance.

"The fuel blasts triggered avalanches," May said. "The snow buried the base like a tomb. If it freezes over, it'll take ages before someone finds the place. There," she pointed out the nearest window. "See for yourself."

Leash tried to sit up . . . *Ouch.* He better not try this again. The sprained back burned like a BBQ grill.

"Easy there," May helped him up, tucking a pillow behind his back. He peered out the nearby window.

The coastline of Greenland stretched thousands of feet below. He could see the mountain range surrounding the bay. The whole basin where the base had stood before now lay buried in a white sarcophagus of giant snowdrifts.

May gazed somberly out the window.

"It will be hard to explain what happened down there."

"Did it?"

She eyed him quizzically. "What do you mean?"

Leash sighed.

"You see . . . the worst part is that Hitch could've been right all along. It all could've been the polar night playing tricks on our minds."

For a long moment they sat in silence, staring at the wilderness below.

Leash knew now was the moment to say it. The thing he'd been planning to say for days. He took a deep breath.

"You know," he said quietly, "when I build my boat, I'll need someone to do the christening."

The pause grew into a pregnant silence. The engines droned gently in the background.

May's voice was equally quiet.

"I'll keep a bottle ready."

They slowly turned toward each other. Their faces drew closer, till their noses nearly touched. It was right then that an odd idea struck Leash. He leaned sideways toward May's neck and pulled her collar aside. The birthmark was there, beckoning him. Quarter-sized, reddish, shaped like Africa. Somewhere in the back of his mind, a stray thought puzzled over this silly image of a tiny Africa hovering above Greenland. He placed a long, tender kiss on the birthmark, then straightened up.

May gaped at him, bewildered, her eyes itching to ask a question. She kept quiet. For that, Leash was grateful. He couldn't possibly have explained why out of all places on her body he chose that stupid blemish. The answer was buried somewhere inside him, but he wasn't going to search for it. Some words are best left inside.

They turned away from each other, forced apart by the awkward pause, and stared out the window. Seen from outside the plane, they looked like a set of strange, turbaned twins gazing through the iced-over windows of their house.

The rescue plane sailed past the bay. It soon crossed the empty sky and vanished on the horizon.

❋ ❋ ❋

A vast snowdrift cut straight across the Arctic land-scape. Far in the distance, glaciers hugged the horizon in a glimmering embrace. Cold winds howled around, raising white, powdery veils. Amid this wilderness, a lone figure jutted from the snow: a rough, clay figure of a man, buried up to his chest. He gazed somberly toward the frozen ocean before him, like Zeus gazing down on Athens from his mountaintop temple. Stuck in his mouth, a scroll with ancient writing flapped in the wind.

A sudden gust of wind blew the writing away.

Printing number
32 10 14 16